LORD LONGSHANKS

Rebecca Ward

FAWCETT CREST • NEW YORK

A Fawcett Crest Book
Published by Ballantine Books
Copyright © 1990 by Maureen Wartski

Library of Congress Catalog Card Number: 90-92920

ISBN 0-449-21806-6

Manufactured in the United States of America

First Edition: June 1990

For Alice Williams

Chapter One

Yoy, oy, oy, bayed the hounds.

Lord Jonathan Longe, third son of the Duke of Parton, glanced over his broad shoulder and saw thirty foxhounds spilling across the top of the down.

Backing his bay stallion into the shade of a thick hawthorn hedge, he stopped to watch the hunt. Under an overcast February sky the hounds were running cleanly. Then came the huntsmen and the whippers-in and the master of the hunt. Even at this distance Lord Burgess had the look of a stuffed capon.

Lord Longe eyed his neighbor disinterestedly. Since he had only lately arrived at his Sussex residence, he did not know much about the short, chubby baronet whose estate abutted Riverway. He had no desire for a closer acquaintance. The Duke of Parton, whose keen wit was both feared and admired in the House of Lords, had dismissed Burgess as a cabbage-head who liked cards and horses too well and had a toad-eating wife.

A high-pitched cry gave the signal that the fox had been viewed. The baying of the hounds became frenzied. Lord Burgess bounced about like an excited red cork. The followers of the hunt urged their mounts forward, and behind them streamed grooms, second horsemen, leading followers, and earth-stoppers.

Lord Longe leaned on the pommel of his saddle and watched the hunt flow up the slope of the next down and disappear from view. Suddenly he whistled.

"What's this?"

A slender youth on a gray gelding was galloping over the down. Bent low, he rode neck-or-nothing in pursuit of the rest of the hunt.

Whoever the boy was, he could ride. Lord Longe watched appreciatively until the newcomer veered away from the beaten path. Then, without slackening speed, he thundered directly toward the hawthorn hedge.

"Hi, you young fool," Lord Longe shouted, "Stop! You'll break your damned neck!"

The rider did not heed the warning, but his gelding apparently had more sense. Just as horse and rider reached the hedge, the animal stopped dead. The youth yelped, flew over the gelding's head, and thudded facedown in the mud.

Cursing, Lord Longe dismounted and ran toward the prone figure. To his relief, the youth was already beginning to stir.

"Are you badly hurt?" he demanded. When the other shook his head, he added roundly, "You deserve to be. Don't try to move right away, young sapskull. That was a rattling fall. Let's see if you've broken something."

"I am persuaded that I have not," the rider said.

Lord Longe started as if he had been stung, for the flushed face that looked up into his was a woman's. As she sat up, the man's bowler she wore fell back, disclosing curls the color of dark honey.

"Is Argos hurt?" she wanted to know. "I will never forgive myself if he has been injured."

Anxious hazel eyes, large and golden and starred with a thick fringe of lashes, met his. Feeling somewhat bemused, Lord Longe replied, "If you mean your horse, he's over there cropping grass."

She turned to look for herself, then drew a deep sigh of relief. "Thank goodness for that. So—all is well. Naturally Seamus will give me a thundering scold, but that cannot be helped."

Her voice was slightly husky, tinged with the same rueful humor that curved her mouth. It was, Lord Longe noted, not the cupid's bow so admired by the stylists of the day, but a warm-lipped, rosy, generous mouth meant for laughter—or for kissing.

With even more interest he studied the girl. She really seemed uninjured by her hard fall, probably because she had landed in a puddle of mud. There was mud all over her breeches and coat, and a patch of mud decorated one rosy cheek. The effect, he had to admit, was charming.

"It was my fault," she was saying contritely. "I should never have tried to take that stitcher of a hedge. And after Aunt Maria expressly forbade me to join the hunt, too. My only excuse is that I had the blue devils, and when they all rode off to hounds this morning, I could not bear to be left behind. So I begged my cousin Freddy to lend me his hunt

3

clothes and bowler and hoped that I might go unnoticed among the others."

Patricia Surrey paused to draw breath. She also wondered at herself. It was not like her to rattle on like this, especially not to an unknown gentleman. He must think that her brains had been addled by the fall.

Who was he? One moment she had been trying to overtake the hunt by using the shortcut that she and her brother Jack had discovered years ago. Then Argos had refused to take the hedge and suddenly here was this tall, broad-shouldered man with the steady gray eyes. Patricia thought, inconsequentially, that she had never seen such clear eyes before. They reminded her of a dawn sky.

She did not need the evidence of his finely cut fawn riding clothes to know that he was a gentleman. His face, framed by thick dark hair told that story. There was that bold cut of nose, the fine lips, and the strong, square chin. That, and his unconscious air of command bespoke years of noble breeding.

He was holding out a hand to help her up. As she took that large, strong hand, Patricia realized for the first time where she had landed. "Oh," she exclaimed, "Freddy will murder me!"

She began to brush wildly at her riding coat. "Freddy is very proud of these clothes—for all that Aunt Maria will never allow him to hunt. And now I have ruined his jacket."

She looked so young in her distress that he couldn't help smiling. "Hunt clothes are meant to be muddied and will mend, believe me."

"Like my pride, sir?" She stopped brushing and smiled at him.

The tentative smile held a question. It also caused a deep dimple to appear in her chin. Lord Longe felt unaccountably dazzled.

"Jonathan Longe, ma'am," he said. "At your service."

"And I am Patricia Surrey. Thank you for hauling me out of the mud, and—" She broke off suddenly, her eyes widened in astonishment, then turned dark with dismay. "Did I hear you say—it *cannot* be that you are the Duke of Parton's son?"

"Alas, that is who I am."

Patricia closed her eyes and shook her head as though to dispel a bad dream. "Aunt will have my head."

He laughed. "First Freddy and now your aunt? You seem to be in mortal danger, Miss Surrey."

"Oh, do not joke—I am really up the River Tick. Your arrival at Riverway has been the talk of the breakfast table for days. Aunt and Uncle Burgess have been most anxious to make your acquaintance."

Jonathan was dumbfounded. This magnificent girl was the cabbage-head's niece!

"Aunt Maria has been beside herself because you have not replied to the invitation she sent you," she continued. "Did you not receive it?"

Vaguely he recalled a card from Lady Burgess requesting his presence at an upcoming rout. He had meant to refuse but had forgotten to do so.

He hedged, "I can't see why our meeting should anger your aunt."

"She is a stickler for etiquette. Riding to hounds is *not* ladylike in her eyes. And if she learns that I met you while I was covered with mud—" She

5

paused a moment then asked hopefully, "But perhaps you will not say anything to her?"

Lord Longe put a hand on his heart. "Word of a gentleman."

She puffed out her cheeks in a relieved sigh. "That is most excessively good of you. And—and if you meet my cousin Delphie, you will not mention the matter to her? She is such a rattle that she might let something slip without meaning to do so. Freddy, of course, will say nothing even if he is furious with me, and Lionel—my oldest cousin—is abroad with my brother, Jack."

It was his turn to look startled. "*Jack* Surrey is your brother?"

"Yes, Captain Jack Surrey of the Nineteenth Foot Guards. Do you know him?"

Her voice was eager, and her eyes were very bright. Lord Longe began to speak then checked himself. "I know him slightly," he said. "He has the reputation of being a gallant gentleman. Is he on furlough, then?"

Her expressive eyes clouded over. "He is newly returned from the Peninsula. He was wounded at Talavera and was sick for a very long time. But he is better now and has gone to Italy with Lionel."

"And you miss him."

"This morning was the worst of all because we used to ride and hunt together."

She turned away, and he knew that she was holding back tears. Lord Longe watched her with a slight frown. Again he began to speak, and once again he thought better of it.

Instead he whistled to her gelding, which came trotting up to him at once. The duke's son ran his hands appreciatively over the horse's neck and face.

6

"Did your brother help you choose this fine fellow?" When she nodded, he went on casually, "How long will he be away in Italy?"

"Three months."

She sounded so sad that Lord Longe turned to look at her. He noted the dimming in her eyes, the anxious tension around her mouth, and found himself wishing he could put his arms around her and comfort her.

Reluctantly he dismissed this improper notion. "A few months isn't an eternity. The time will pass quickly."

"That is what Aunt Maria tells me. She has been most kind, really, and this rout is meant to cheer me. But I would much rather—"

"You would much rather be riding to hounds," he suggested and was rewarded by another of those dazzling smiles.

"You have found me out. When Jack was away at war, I rode a great deal. It is idiotish, I know, but I felt closest to him when I was on a horse."

She turned away and looked yearningly over the green down. He watched in silence thinking that he must definitely send a card to Lady Burgess accepting her invitation. He also considered the absent Captain Jack Surrey.

Suddenly Patricia raised her head. "The fox must have doubled," she exclaimed. "The hounds are coming back this way." She turned back to the tall man and held out her hand. "I must get back to Burgess Hall before I am seen," she said frankly. "Thank you for coming to my rescue and—and for agreeing not to say anything to my aunt and uncle."

Holding the small hand in its muddy glove, he

smiled down at her. "In return for my remaining as silent as the grave, will you allow me a waltz?"

"Then you are coming to the rout? Aunt Maria will be delighted."

"And the waltz?" he prompted.

"Indeed I will be glad to dance with you, sir." Her voice was demure, but her eyes danced as she added, "And I collect that it will be safe for you to do so, seeing that there will not be any hedges and mud puddles for *miles* around."

He held her horse for her as she mounted and approved the sure way she sat her saddle and gathered up the reins. The momentary shadows in her eyes had gone, and the smile she gave him was jaunty. She spurred the gelding forward and moments later was cantering back the way she had come.

The duke's son watched the sun glint richly against Patricia Surrey's hair. He recalled how her eyes turned golden when she smiled and thought of the dimple that accentuated her lips.

Then he thought of her brother again. He frowned.

"Damnation," he murmured. "That is going to be awkward."

Just then Patricia topped the down. She turned to wave at him, and as he returned her salute, Lord Longe's brow cleared.

"Surrey won't be back in England for a while," he told himself. "I'll have enough time."

Chapter Two

"Sure, and didn't I warn you against this cockle-brained idea, Argos?" Seamus fumed.

Patricia had managed to ride up to the stables undetected, but she hadn't been able to escape her groom. When he saw her, Seamus's tufts of white hair fairly stood on end, and his leathery face puckered up into a thunderous scowl.

"It's not decent, Argos, to be riding to hounds dressed like a man. The late master and mistress, God rest them, will be turning in their graves."

One of Seamus's most maddening traits was that he would never scold Patricia directly. All his comments were aimed at her gelding. In fact, his faded blue eyes glared at a point between the beast's ears.

Patricia slid out of the saddle and said in a conciliatory tone, "I know that it was not quite the thing, but I did so want to ride to hounds." Seamus sniffed. "Besides, no harm has been done."

"No harm is it, with yourself in a lather, Argos,

and mud all over Miss Patricia? Musha, musha, it's plain that she rode at a high hedge—again."

Patricia attempted a repressive glare. It was a total failure. Seamus led the gelding away complaining, "And to think that her ladyship's entertaining fine guests. What will they think, Argos, if they see Miss Patricia in Mr. Harmon's riding clothes?"

"What guests?" but the maddening old fellow would not answer. "Oh, hell and the devil," Patricia exclaimed, and had the satisfaction of seeing Seamus wince.

Using Jack's favorite oath made her feel quite cheerful, and Patricia was humming as she walked toward the house. Burgess Hall had been built in the time of the Tudors and should have appeared imposing, but succeeded only in appearing cluttered. Its towers, dormers, and turrets had a haphazard look as if its builder had slapped everything together in a hurry. The garden path along which Patricia walked was almost choked with flowers, topiary bushes, and shrubs.

The house had no less than three side doors. Patricia swung one of these open and glanced warily about her, but there was nobody in the ground floor anteroom except for several Burgess ancestors who gazed disapprovingly from their gilt frames. The Venetian mirror hung near the curving staircase reflected an image that made her wince, however. Hunting hat jammed down over her curls, coat and breeches covered with mud—no wonder Seamus had scolded.

Patricia was making for the stairs when an irate voice behind her cried, "I s-say, Pat, d-dash it all!"

Inwardly she groaned. "Hello, Freddy."

"D-don't you 'hello Freddy' me," her cousin spluttered.

Freddy Harmon's usually mild blue eyes were snapping with righteous anger. His longish face, often compared by his fond father to that of a ruminative sheep's, burned indignantly.

"D-doing it too brown, Pat," he accused. "B-borrowing my new hunt clothes, and r-ruining them."

"I do not wonder that you are angry," Patricia soothed. "But you see, I was behind everyone, and there was this hedge. I thought I could take it clean and catch up to the others."

Her eyes sparkled at the memory, and Freddy regarded his older cousin with reluctant admiration. "D-did you?"

She threw her arms wide in rueful denial. "Argos stopped dead, and I went over his head."

"And landed in the m-mud," Freddy tried to grumble, but he had begun to grin. "I hope nobody saw you m-making a cake of yourself, Pat."

Patricia recalled gray eyes that held both concern and amusement and the clasp of a strong hand. Involuntarily she smiled. "Do not worry, Freddy," she said. "I will clean your clothes until they are as good as new."

Freddy heaved a sigh that seemed to originate in his boots. "It don't matter anyhow," he mumbled. "I'll never wear them. Mama'll never let me ride to hounds."

Patricia reflected that this was very likely true. Freddy had been sickly as a baby, and his mother was still convinced that her younger son would be snatched away by some lurking fever or accident. Freddy was forbidden to exercise, walk outside in

11

cold weather, or come near a horse. Lady Burgess also supervised her son's diet and encouraged his valet to spy on him.

Patricia loathed the burly and mean-eyed Mimsby. She was not alone. The Burgess servants, who knew that he bullied his master, spoke impertinently to him, and consistently made his life miserable, would have been glad to see the last of the valet. But Mimsby was crafty, fed Lady Burgess's anxieties, and continued high in her favor.

Freddy was too meek to complain about Mimsby's treatment. And since he dreaded his mother's histrionics, he usually gave way to her whims. For example, today he was wearing a heavy waistcoat of wool, which he hated, under his new double-breasted coat of fine-faced cloth.

Recalling what Seamus had said, she wondered, "Who has come to call?"

"Oh, d-damn it, I forgot," Freddy exclaimed. "They're all in the morning room, and M-Mama's waiting for me." He began to scurry up the stairs then paused to warn, "M-Mama's been asking for you, too, Pat. If she c-catches you dressed in my clothes, she'll kick up no end of d-dust."

This awful thought was enough to lend wings to Patricia's heels. She ran up three flights of stairs without stopping and, with the help of her abigail, made short work of dressing. Within ten minutes her hair had been braided à la Didion, and she had changed Freddy's muddied riding coat and breeches for a peach-colored muslin day dress.

She was putting the final touches to her toilette when there was a knock on the door and a thin, middle-aged lady in green bombazine peered in.

"Ah, Miss Surrey," she exclaimed coyly. "At last!"

Politely Patricia replied, "Good morning, Miss Wigge."

The thin lady fluttered into the room. She then glanced at her reflection in the mirror and paused to smooth the emerald-green fringe trim that gave her dress the illusion of a bust.

"Her ladyship has sent me to find you," she announced. "She wishes you to come downstairs to be introduced to Colonel Waldo Charteris."

"Ah, the mystery guest," Patricia murmured.

"He is Lord and Lady Burgess's new neighbor. His estate lies to the west of us. He is a man of Mars home on furlough from the grim fields of battle." Miss Wigge struck a dramatic pose and quoted, " 'And bold and hard adventures t'undertake,/ Leaving his county for his country's sake,' as Fitzgerald says. Hem! And there is also Burke. 'So to be patriots, as not to forget we are gentlemen.' "

Conversing with Delphie's governess was rather like walking through fog. Patricia said, somewhat hastily, that since her aunt had requested her presence, she should go down.

Miss Wigge threw back her head and clasped her hands to her fringed bosom. "Yes, go with all haste, for with the colonel has come Adonis. Were I younger, Miss Surrey—but soft. Some things are best unsaid. Adieu, ma'am."

She flitted out of the room and left Patricia to make her way to the morning room. As she descended to the second floor, she could hear a murmur of conversation. Then one loud, hectoring male voice rose above the others.

"That's what's needed by the army—old-fashioned discipline. I said as much to Sir Arthur Wellesley the other day. 'Sir Arthur,' I said, 'the problem with his majesty's armies is a lack of discipline."

Patricia turned the doorknob of the morning room and went in. The self-important voice stopped short as she said, "I am sorry to be late."

Smiling, she glanced about a room that should have been comfortable had it not been crammed to the bursting point with furniture, bric-a-brac, and curios. Large gilt-bronze figures rubbed close shoulders with marble statuary, a jardiniere overflowing with roses, and a tea tray that reposed on an Indian brass table.

There were several people in the room. Freddy was leaning against a fireplace of Carrara marble. His older sister Delphinium, looking excessively pretty in a sprigged muslin morning dress with puffed sleeves, perched on a chair by the wall. Tall Lady Burgess had spread the skirts of her yellow walking-out dress over the edges of a Chinese Chippendale daybed. With her graying fair hair, high forehead, and pale blue eyes, she had the look of a hopeful rabbit. Near her stood two gentlemen in regimentals.

"There you are at last, my dear," Lady Burgess exclaimed eagerly. "Colonel, this is my niece, Miss Patricia Surrey. My love, this is Colonel Waldo Charteris."

The larger of the two military gentlemen bowed stiffly. He had a bullet-shaped head covered with sandy hair and no neck to speak of. Slightly protuberant greenish eyes surveyed Patricia out of a florid, rectangular face bisected by a flaring mustache.

"Miss Surrey, your most obedient," he trumpeted.

Gravely Patricia curtsied.

"Permit me to introduce my aide and secretary," the colonel continued in the same stentorian tones. "This is Captain Farell."

Patricia blinked. For once Miss Wigge had not been exaggerating. Seldom had she seen such a handsome man.

Captain Farell's brown hair waved romantically about his fine forehead. His eyes were large, dark, and expressive. He had a beautifully chiseled nose, sensuous lips, and a cleft chin. The scarlet regimental tunic fitted his slender form like a glove.

"Servant, ma'am—assure you, greatest pleasure," the captain exclaimed.

He bowed awkwardly, then straightened to wooden attention. Patricia was slightly disappointed. A man who looked like the hero out of a fairy tale should, she thought, be blessed with a voice and manners to match his appearance.

"Pray sit down, my dear, and take some refreshment." Lady Burgess waved a vague hand toward the tea tray. "Colonel Charteris has been so obliging as to explain how things stand on the Peninsula."

Patricia sat down beside Delphie, who whispered, "Patricia, is he not wondrously handsome?"

Seeing that her cousin's amethyst eyes were fastened on Captain Farell, Patricia teased, "As handsome as Romeo, perhaps?"

Delphie clasped her hands. "He is even more handsome than poor Signor Montefiori."

Remembering what Freddy had once written to her about his sister's short-lived tender for her Italian dancing master, Patricia hid a smile. Lord Burgess had made short work of *that* situation, but then there had been the curate with the beautiful, classic head and the penniless poet with the 'lovely blue eyes'—

"Patricia, my love," Lady Burgess was saying, "are you rainbow-chasing? The colonel has asked you a question."

"Lady Burgess tells me that your brother's regiment was the Nineteenth Foot Guards." When Patricia assented, the colonel smoothed his mustache and announced, "I am an artillery man myself and have, if I may so say, some experience in the art of war."

According to him, he knew everyone of importance in London and on the Peninsula. He was intimate with all the generals. He was—this was natural, he explained, since his brother was the Viscount Teglare—on a friendly footing with the most important peers in London.

"I have also," boomed the colonel, "recently executed a commission for Sir Arthur Wellesley—though I should now give him his new title of Viscount Wellington. It was his lordship who insisted that I take a furlough before returning to my duties. 'Charteris, you've earned a rest,' he told me. Those were his very words."

"D-did you know my cousin Jack, sir?" Freddy asked eagerly, as the colonel paused to draw breath. "I mean, p-personally. He was wounded at Talavera."

"Ah, Talavera." Colonel Charteris produced a silver snuffbox and helped himself liberally. "That was a day for heroes, young man. Fifty thousand Frenchies against half that number of Englishmen.

But one Englishman is worth a dozen frogs as anyone knows. My former aide, Captain Philip Oranger, fell before enemy fire. The cannonade from our great guns was horrible—*my* gunners did their duty. But I must apologize. Such matters are too gruesome for the fair ears of the fair."

"On the contrary," Patricia exclaimed, "I for one would be very interested to hear more."

The colonel took more snuff. "The enemy fought like fiends. There were terrible salvos of fire against our men. But the 'thin red line' held, and every Englishman did his duty. All, that is, except for one cowardly officer who ran in the face of fire."

"Who was this c-coward, sir?" Freddy cried.

The colonel shook his head. "It would serve no purpose to divulge his name, but I shall say this. Because their officer turned and fled, his men became confused and were easily cut down by French fire. He caused the death of many men. The blood of the Nineteenth Foot Guard is on his head."

There were exclamations of horror from Lady Burgess and Delphie, but Patricia sat in stricken silence. If not for this craven wretch, Jack would not have been wounded.

Captain Farell coughed and said, "I wasn't at Talavera myself—not yet in the colonel's service—but I heard the talk." He caught his superior's impatient eye and continued hastily, "Heard that the, ah, officer in question was connected to persons in high places. Incident smoothed over to spare them embarrassment—noblesse oblige, don't you know."

"Someone should have shot the villain!" Patricia cried.

"My dear," Lady Burgess protested, but the colonel smiled approvingly.

"I couldn't have put it better myself. The bas—er, the fellow should have been horsewhipped. But as I have said before, the military is not what it used to be. I said as much to Sir Arthur—I mean, his lordship the Viscount Wellington, the other day. 'Sir Arthur,' I said, 'what is needed here is a strong hand.' And he replied, 'Charteris, you are right.' Which proves my point exactly—"

He launched into another long-winded monologue, but Patricia paid scant attention. She was thinking of the coward who had nearly caused Jack's death. Who was he? *Where* was he at this moment?

Patricia clenched her hands into tight fists. If she had one prayer, she thought passionately, it would be to someday meet the dastard face-to-face.

"Oh, Wiggy, is he not here *yet*?"

Miss Wigge, encased in a plum-colored gown that had seen better years, turned slightly from her station at the window and reproved, "Miss Delphinium, calm yourself, I beg. Remember that they also serve, who only stand and wait."

"I hate to wait," Delphie sighed.

She twirled experimentally on her dainty slippers, and Patricia surveyed her cousin with admiration. Delphie's silver gauze dress over a slip of palest rose complimented her peach bloom loveliness. The pearls she wore around her neck were the perfect foil for her creamy skin. In her golden hair, tonight dressed in the Grecian style, Delphie wore pink silk roses.

"You look like a fairy-tale princess," Patricia smiled.

"I hope *he* thinks so. I am persuaded that Captain Farell is an extremely sensitive gentleman. While the colonel prosed on and on, we exchanged *such* speaking looks—"

A shriek from Miss Wigge interrupted her. " 'Oh, Young Lochinvar is come out of the west!' "

Delphie sped to the window and peered over her governess's shoulder. "Do you think he will waltz with me tonight, Patricia?" she breathed.

"Of all the m-maggoty n-notions." Freddy had stopped at his sister's open doorway. "H-how would anyone know what Farell's going to do?"

Delphie started to stick out her tongue at her younger brother, then caught herself and tossed her curls in a dignified way. "We will see what we will see."

Nose tilted to the skies, she swept by Freddy and, attended by Miss Wigge, glided gracefully down the stairs. Freddy looked after her in disgust.

"Of all the c-cabbage-brained females—she's up to one of her starts again. S-someone should warn that poor b-bleater, Farell."

He started down the hall, and Patricia fell into step with him. "He seems a pleasant young man, which is more than I can say about Colonel Waldo Charteris."

"P-pompous ass," Freddy agreed. "But M-Mama don't think so. Farell don't have a feather to fly with nor c-connections neither. Third son of a country gentleman, or s-some such thing, while Charteris is as rich as Golden Ball and has g-got a brother who's a viscount. Mama thinks it would be a g-good thing if someone as 'settled' as Charteris would come courting Delphie. But Charteris ain't s-settled. He's c-congealed."

They had come down the stairs to the first floor

anteroom where a small orchestra was playing for the pleasure of the guests. Gorgeously liveried footmen stood at attention by the door of the drawing room.

Freddy regarded this chamber with a scowl. "I h-hate these b-beastly affairs," he mumbled. "Don't mind t-telling you, Pat, wish I could do a b-bolt."

Patricia felt a rush of sympathy. She knew that her cousin loathed these gatherings. He was shy, and conversing with so many people made him stutter so badly that he could scarcely be understood.

"Well, I do not blame you," she said frankly. "I, too, mislike meeting so many people all at once." As Freddy nodded glumly, she added, "I have a suggestion. Let us stay together and *ease* ourselves into the company by stages."

Freddy was relieved and grateful, but his pride would not allow him to admit this. He picked an imaginary piece of lint from his coat and said gruffly, "If it'll h-help *you*, Pat, I'm up to the m-mark."

He offered her his arm, and she took it. Then, as they entered the drawing room together she exclaimed, "Aunt Maria must have invited everyone in the county."

The handsome, oblong room was full of people. Gentlemen, resplendent in their finely cut frock coats, embroidered satin waistcoats, starched shirt frills, and tight breeches, regaled each other with anecdotes of the hunt or racing or gaming. The older gentlemen eyed the trays of claret and sherry that were being offered by the Burgess's servants, while the younger men cast speaking glances at the young ladies.

Under the watchful eye of their mamas, aunts, or guardians, these young ladies talked and giggled among themselves all the while taking their admirers' measure. Light from the crystal chandeliers danced over their rainbow silks, watered satins, and figured laces. Diamonds flashed on white bosoms. Rubies blazed on slender wrists. Wreaths of flowers and seed pearls and gold nets sparkling with gems crowned golden or titian or dark curls.

In the midst of this cheerful confusion Patricia could see no sign of a tall, broad-shouldered man with clear gray eyes. Lord Longe had not come, after all. She felt unaccountably disappointed.

"Oh, b-blast," Freddy groaned. "There's Charteris with the p-pater. They're c-coming this way."

A wall of crimson was advancing toward them. "Miss Surrey, how well you look," the colonel brayed.

Did the man always have to shout? Patricia tried not to wince as her hand was seized and wrung painfully.

"You do look well, m'dear." Lord Burgess had trotted up in the colonel's wake. "And I see you brought my son with you. Well, well, there you are at last, sir. Needed your hand held, hey?"

Her uncle's brand of humor always made Patricia feel uneasy. "The shoe is on the other foot, Uncle Hector," she said. "Freddy is giving me countenance among your guests."

"Oh, fol rol. Freddy couldn't give countenance to a goose. And you ain't afraid of anything, Patricia." Lord Burgess winked at the colonel and added, "Just like m'late brother, God rest him. Game as a pebble, hey?"

He turned to his son and advised him to keep near to his cousin so that some of her pluck would rub off on him. Patricia did not hear Freddy's reply, for Colonel Waldo Charteris was leaning toward her.

"I am told that there is to be dancing, and I'd take it as a favor, ma'am, if you saved a cotillion for me. I am," he added complacently, "partial to the cotillion. No less a personage than the Duchess of Braeford has remarked on my skill in that dance. 'Colonel,' her grace told me, 'I have never seen the cotillion performed with such address.' "

Patricia was saved from the necessity of answering by her uncle, who desired the colonel to join a group of gentlemen standing nearby. Freddy watched their departure bitterly.

"The pater's g-gaming friends," he told Patricia. "C-cards and horses—that's all they think about. "I'll lay you a monkey that he's going to set up a game with the colonel—oh, Lord, now M-Mama's seen us."

Lady Burgess was indeed signaling to them. Patricia gave her cousin's arm a squeeze. "Heart up, Freddy," she whispered. "Remember, we stand together."

Together they crossed the room. Freddy, looking resigned, underwent a cross-examination concerning his health while Patricia began a conversation with two of her aunt's neighbors. One was Lady Yancey, a plump, matter-of-fact soul who was full of the doings of her husband, her three sons, and their many horses and hounds. The other was Lady Were.

Patricia had met Lady Were once before. Her ladyship had the sharp features of a ferret and a

22

deceptively silky voice in which she contrived to ask a hundred intimate questions and drop as many sly hints about those present. She also implied that it was a good thing that Lady Yancey's youngest son, Percival, was coming down from London.

"For I have heard," Lady Were said in her poisonously sweet voice, "that the set in which he moves is forever roistering about at Vauxhall, or breaking shop windows, or being fleeced in gambling halls around Jermyn Street."

Lady Yancey said mildly that she was sure this was not so. "Percy is too lazy to engage in such behavior. Besides, gambling bores him."

"Would that were true of all people." Lady Were lowered her voice to add gently, "I understand, for instance, that our host has recently lost a small fortune on a horse that did not even show. I collect that *dear* Maria must be grateful that he is rusticating at present. One cannot lose one's entire fortune in the country."

Patricia was grateful when her aunt drew her aside.

"My dear, I must ask a favor of you," Lady Burgess said. "Will you be so obliging as to take Freddy and go and sit with Delphinium? Miss Wigge is nearby, but I fear that she is not always an adequate chaperon."

Patricia followed her aunt's gaze and saw that Delphie was seated in a small, curtained alcove. Captain Farell was standing very close to her, and they appeared to be deep in conversation. Seated a few feet away was the beaming Miss Wigge.

The governess looked somewhat guilty as Patricia and Freddy approached and murmured something unintelligible about youth. Delphie interrupted her to say, "I am glad you are here. Captain Farell has been telling us such heroic stories."

The captain looked embarrassed and said somewhat stiffly, "Too kind, Miss Harmon. Afraid I've been prosing on and on—boring stuff."

He smoothed his cutaway scarlet tunic and stood rocking back and forth on his bootheels while Delphie enthused, "But that is not so. I love hearing about heroes, and so do my cousin and brother. Do sit down, both of you, and listen to Captain Farell, both of you."

Freddy preferred to stand so that he could hide in the shadow of the curtains. Patricia took the seat next to Delphie and said, "Pray continue, Captain."

Thus encouraged, the captain plunged into the description of a military campaign. His abrupt, jerky style of talking somehow suited the charge that he was describing, and as he spoke of the heroic deeds of English officers, Freddy forgot his shyness, Miss Wigge confessed herself ready to swoon, and Delphie clasped her hands to her bosom.

Patricia was as spellbound as the others. At one point she closed her eyes and imagined Jack heroically fighting off a force of Frenchmen. Indeed, she could almost feel herself there *with* him.

"I wish," a deep voice said, "that all of that were true."

Patricia's eyes flew open, for she recognized that voice. She turned quickly, a smile on her lips.

Not so Captain Farell, who grated, "What's that, sir?"

Lord Longe had, Patricia noted, dressed for the occasion in a dove-gray frock coat so impeccably tailored that it fit his powerful shoulders like a second skin. His tight-fitting breeches revealed an athlete's muscled legs. His snowy-white cravat had been simply but meticulously arranged and glinted with a diamond stickpin. Gray eyes, the color of a dawn sky, smiled down into hers.

Lord Longe had thought he carried a picture of Patricia Surrey with him these past days, but now he knew that the memory was inadequate. Tonight Patricia wore a slender dress of amber silk; high-waisted and unadorned except for a banding of fine lace. She wore no jewels save for a golden chain around her throat. A single tea rose was tucked into honey-rich curls that she wore in the Roman style.

She was, Lord Longe realized, unlike any woman he had known before. Her vivid loveliness did not need fashionable artifices like frills and laces and corsets that pinched in or pushed up parts of the female anatomy. She did not need gewgaws or jewels. Like the rose in her hair, she was perfect and complete.

He almost blurted a greeting before recalling that, as far as anyone knew, Lord Longe and Miss Surrey had not yet met.

"Allow me to introduce myself," he said. "I am Jonathan Longe."

He was interrupted by a squeak from Delphie. "The Duke of Parton's son!" She quickly collected herself and added primly, "How do you do, my lord. I am Miss Harmon, and this is my cousin, Miss Surrey, and my younger brother, Freddy, and my governess, Miss Wigge. And this gentleman is Captain Farell, who is secretary and aide to Colonel Charteris."

Lord Longe gravely acknowledged each introduction. He bowed to Delphie and Miss Wigge, then shook Freddy's hand. But when he came to Patricia, he could not resist saying, "Forgive me, Miss Surrey, but is it possible that we have met before this?"

"Alas, I cannot say that we have," she replied demurely.

"P-perhaps, my lord, you know her b-brother Jack," Freddy ventured eagerly, but was silenced by the captain.

"Lord Longe," he said ominously, "Must insist, sir—do you consider me a liar?"

He glared at Lord Longe, who replied calmly, "I do not. You spoke of war as you see it. My perception of it is different, that is all."

"And what, pray, do you know of war?"

The captain's question bordered on insolence. Lord Longe's eyebrow slanted up, but he answered equably. "For a brief time I held a commission as major in the Nineteenth Foot Guard."

Patricia cried out in astonishment, and Freddy exclaimed, "But that is J-Jack's regiment!"

The captain was also looking surprised. "Excellent regiment—heroic, don't you know. Should be proud, sir—can't understand your sentiments."

"There's little to understand. I found war unpleasant, tedious, and deadly. To romanticize it is folly."

Farell scowled. Delphie wore a puzzled expression. Freddy said confusedly, "B-but there are so many st-stories about b-brave m-men in the war. My co-cousin J-Jack, for instance, is a f-fine sh-shot and a cl-clipping g-good r-r—a g-g-g-"

He lapsed into stammering incoherence. Captain Farell looked embarrassed, but Lord Longe spoke as though nothing was amiss. "Yes, I'm sure he's

26

an excellent rider. And you yourself must have a liking for horses."

Freddy took in a gulp of air and opened his mouth. Nothing came out. He turned beet red and nodded miserably.

"In that case perhaps you'll come to Riverway and take a look at my hunters," Lord Longe said.

Freddy was so pleased that he found his tongue again. "I would l-like that above all things," he cried. "M-may I really?"

"I hope you will. We're neighbors, after all."

The orchestra had followed the guests into the drawing room, and the strains of a waltz now rose over the sounds of laughter and conversation. As guests began to position themselves to dance, Lord Longe bowed and requested that Patricia honor him with a waltz.

She offered him her hand and as he led her to the floor said, "Why did you not tell me at once that your regiment was the same as my brother's?"

Her last words were somewhat breathless, for she was being whirled onto the drawing room floor. It was not the dance itself that had this effect on her, but the reality of being held in Lord Longe's strong embrace. Though the regulation twelve inches separated them, she had the feeling that his encircling arms were holding her much more closely than was proper.

With some difficulty she continued. "I collect that you said that you are no longer with the guards. Were you wounded as Jack was?"

"I sold out some months ago."

Something in his voice troubled her, and she drew her delicate brows together.

"War is terrible, of course," she murmured.

"When Jack was sent to the Peninsula, I wanted so badly to go with him and take care of him. I worried about him constantly. I could only bear it because I knew he was fighting to keep England free."

He wondered what she would think if he told her that six thousand Englishmen had been killed between Astorga and Corunna, that fifty-three hundred lay dead at Talavera, and that many more had been wounded. But this was not conversation fit for a lady's ears.

Lord Longe smiled down at the woman in his arms. "You waltz beautifully, ma'am."

He didn't wish to discuss the war. Patricia thought she understood. She felt that Lord Longe must have suffered terribly and wished to wipe all memories from his mind.

With some effort she matched his light tone. "My brother taught me to dance," she explained. "I must tell you that he was not a patient teacher. Many, many times I was raked over the coals for treading on his feet, and once I thought he would box my ears."

Lord Longe watched the dimple tease Patricia's chin. He also saw the shadows that lingered in her eyes as she spoke of her brother. He said, "I have brothers, too, but we are not as close. I envy you."

"We lost our parents some years ago," she replied quietly. "Our aunt and uncle were kind to us, but we were most often alone at our home in Somerset. And—and even when Jack was away on the Peninsula, I felt somehow that we were together."

She tried to make herself sound matter-of-fact and cheerful, but her voice held a wistful loneliness. Lord Longe wanted to draw her close and comfort her, but he no longer had an excuse to do so.

The strains of the music had come to an end, and his lordship knew that he could not continue to stand in the middle of the drawing room floor holding Patricia in his arms.

As he reluctantly stepped away from her, she exclaimed impulsively, "How I wish that Jack were here. I am persuaded that you would deal famously together."

An odd look filled his eyes for a moment. Then, wordlessly, he raised her hand to his lips.

Patricia felt the caress of Lord Longe's lips through her glove. The warmth of that kiss traversed her hand and arm and seemed to settle about her heart. She gave herself a mental shake and tried to regain her balance. *What is the matter with you, wigeon?*

There was a cough at her elbow, and a loud voice brayed, "Miss Surrey, will you permit me to lead you to the floor?"

Somewhat dazedly, Patricia turned her head and looked into Colonel Charteris's flushed countenance. "They are taking their places for the cotillion," the colonel explained smugly.

A strong smell of spirits accompanied his words. His smile was bleary. Lord Longe felt the small hand he still held grow tense and knew she didn't want to dance with this lout.

"I regret, sir," he said smoothly, "that Miss Surrey has promised the cotillion to me."

The colonel frowned. His cheeks grew mottled with displeasure. "Eh, what? What did you say?"

Patricia watched Lord Longe's dark eyebrow slant up. Centuries of hauteur and *noblesse oblige* flashed in his eyes. "I *said*, sir, that Miss Surrey has promised the cotillion to me."

There was ice in his voice, and his eyes were like chips of frozen granite. Patricia thought that a man would have to be mad to argue with such eyes or such a voice.

But the colonel's enormous conceit made him immune to common sense. He glared at the interloper and barked, "And who might you be?"

Patricia spoke quickly to prevent an open quarrel. "Lord Longe," she said, "I collect that you are not acquainted with Colonel Waldo Charteris? Colonel, this gentleman is Lord Longe." She paused and added for good measure, "the Duke of Parton's son."

It was rather like watching a convulsion pass through an elephant. The colonel stared. He went pale, his eyelids narrowed, and his mustache seemed to quiver like the antennae of a beetle. He looked very closely at the tall man before him and then, without so much as another word, turned on his heel and stalked away.

"Of all the rag-mannered things to do," Patricia exclaimed.

"I imagine that the colonel is a man used to having his own way." Jonathan spoke calmly, but the hard look remained in his eyes. "Has he been bothering you?"

She shook her head. "Colonel Charteris is too ridiculous to bother anyone. My cousin Freddy calls him a pompous ass." She frowned. "I should not have said that."

"Your cousin is a wise man." Jonathan offered Patricia his arm. "Well, Miss Surrey, shall it be the cotillion? Or perhaps you are tired and would prefer some refreshment."

Patricia glanced toward her aunt. She knew that

Lady Burgess would be scandalized if her niece danced twice in succession with the same gentleman. And there would be talk. Several matrons, anxious to advance their own daughters' cause with the extremely eligible Lord Longe, were staring disapprovingly at Patricia, and Lady Were had the happy, absorbed look of one who scents a new source of impropriety.

She should not dance the cotillion with Lord Longe, Patricia knew. She also realized that she wanted to do so. He had been kind to Freddy. He had rescued her from the odious colonel. Besides, she liked his company—and the smile in his gray eyes.

They were smiling down at her now. Patricia drew a deep breath and mentally snapped her fingers in the face of convention.

"By all means," she declared, "let it be the cotillion."

Chapter Three

"**O**f all the maggoty ideas," Freddy fumed. "Lord Longe's b-bound to think us rag-mannered if we b-barge in on him like this."

Complacently Lady Burgess settled her violet-colored pelisse and adjusted the egret feather in her bonnet. "Pray do not enact me a Cheltenham tragedy, my son. Neighbors call upon one another every day."

Delphie, who was coming down the stairs with Patricia, said in her most grown-up voice, "Little boys can be *so* tiresome."

Her brother begged her to take a damper, and Patricia interrupted to keep peace, "What Freddy means, perhaps, is that Lord Longe did not actually invite us to Riverway Place."

"What's this, hey?"

Lord Burgess was also descending the stairs. With the help of a corset and the buckram padding in his shoulders, his lordship looked to be in the kick of fashion. His square-tailed plum-colored coat was cut in the Brummell fashion, his collar points rose high against his round cheeks, and he wore close-fitting pantaloons of a canary yellow.

He trotted down the stairs, and a strong perfume, reputed to be the rage in London, wafted after him.

"Are we ready, hey?" he demanded. "Won't be there for tea if we don't get a move on. What's this argle-bargle I've been hearing?"

"Freddy," Lady Burgess sighed, "seems to think that we might be *persona non grata* at Riverway Place."

Lord Burgess gave his son a disgusted look. "Fustian. Longe invited me to see his hunters."

"He invited *m-me*," Freddy protested.

His fond parent laughed. "Spare me, boy. You don't know the front of a horse from its backside. Well, Maria? Are we going or ain't we?"

He took his curly beaver from a footman, offered his lady his arm, and marched through the door. Delphie paused only to check her reflection in the mirror before following her parents.

Freddy muttered, "I hate it. Lord Longe was so damned d-decent, and now M-Mama will toad-eat him, and the pater will make st-stupid jokes, and he'll wish us all in J-Jericho." He paused before adding bitterly, "I tell you, Pat, sometimes I want to t-tell them to go to Jericho myself."

Patricia wished it were permissible to shake one's uncle and aunt. "Perhaps you should," she said warmly. "At least, you might try standing up to Uncle Hector. I am persuaded that he would not browbeat you so if you showed some—some fight, Freddy."

"Stand up to him!" Her cousin gave a laugh that

was also a sob, and Lady Burgess stopped dead in her tracks.

"Was that a cough, Freddy?" she demanded. "Mimsby warned me that you had sneezed this morning, and I am persuaded that your cloak is not warm enough. Get into the carriage at once and cover yourself with this rug. The putrid throat is rife these days—"

"D-dash it, Mama," Freddy began, but Lady Burgess quelled him with a look.

"Perhaps you would prefer to stay at home, my son?"

Freddy's shoulders slumped and the fight drained out of him. Watching, Patricia wished she could also shake Freddy.

She was silent as she followed her cousin into the carriage. Lord Burgess now mounted his horse, and the party started forward. Afternoon sunlight filtered through tall chestnut trees as they traversed the road that led toward the downs.

Ten minutes later they crested the first down and looked across a rolling Sussex countryside composed of wooded hills, meadows, and streams. In the distance were orchards and farms. These were bare now, but soon they would be green with Spring. In the distance they could glimpse the village of Pelham-on-Wye and the spire of an old Norman church.

Lord Burgess led the way to a fork in the road. Toward the east lay Riverway Place, a gracious country estate with a house set against the tree-shaded Leads River. Some distance along the westerly road stood Colonel Charteris's establishment, a rectangular, brownstone building set squarely in the midst of a huge estate.

The coachman had barely turned the horses onto the road toward Riverway when Delphie uttered a shriek. "Oh, heavens—look! Higgins, do stop the horses at once!"

The startled coachman complied and Lord Burgess, who had been riding a little ahead, turned around to see what was happening.

A solitary rider in scarlet regimentals was cantering toward them. "I believe that it is Captain Farell," Patricia exclaimed.

"He is coming to Burgess Hall, and we are not there," Delphie murmured tragically.

"Well, he can leave his card, can't he?" Lord Burgess demanded. "Don't be a peagoose, girl. Higgins, drive on."

As the coachman clicked his team into motion, Delphie cried, "Higgins, I demand that you stop immediately!"

For a second time, the team came to a jarring halt. Lady Burgess was thrown against Patricia and Freddy exclaimed, "Dash it, D-Delphie, m-make up your beastly mind, will you? All this jerking's enough to m-make a fellow d-dizzy."

Lady Burgess was horrified. She demanded that Freddy lie down and put up his feet while her husband, complaining that he was saddled with a family of cockle-brained want-wits, commanded the coachman to drive on.

"But, Papa," Delphie pointed out, "Captain Farell may have an important message for you and Mama—perhaps—perhaps an invitation from the colonel."

Lord Burgess frowned. "Something in that," he allowed. "Stop the damned horses, Higgins. We'll wait a minute. Hey, Maria?"

Lady Burgess, who was propping a pillow under Freddy's knees, did not respond, but Delphie was delighted. "Is he not *wonderful?*" she whispered to Patricia. "He looks just like a knight of old."

Patricia had to admit that the captain cut a fine figure on a horse. As he drew closer, he snapped to attention and saluted. "Trust I'm not detaining you?" he began.

Lord Burgess tapped his riding crop on the pommel of his saddle. "Matter of fact, you are," he said bluntly. "We're making for Riverway."

Patricia saw an indescribable expression flicker in the young officer's eyes. "I beg your pardon, sir," he then said stiffly, "but I have been charged with delivering this letter."

Lord Burgess took the proffered letter, opened the seal, and grunted with satisfaction. "The colonel's inviting me to sit down to cards with him this very night. Yancey and his sons will be there. And we've been asked to 'an evening with a few friends' next week. Hey? What think you of that, Maria?"

Forgetting Freddy for the moment, Lady Burgess beamed. "How very kind of the colonel. We will send an answer immediately—" she broke off as she saw the way Delphie was dimpling at the captain and added repressively, "Thank you, Captain Farell. Now we must be on our way."

But the young officer didn't take the hint. "Permit me to accompany you," he exclaimed.

Freddy groaned. "Oh, m-my God. Do we have to t-take *him* to Riverway, too?"

"We cannot very well be rude to the colonel's aide." But Lady Burgess was not pleased. She had seen *that look* in Delphinium's eyes, and she knew her daughter. She also knew that a gentleman without connections or fortune was not an acceptable suitor for any young miss.

Critically she surveyed Delphie. The girl was very pretty. She had an alabaster brow, amethyst eyes, a rosebud mouth—and golden curls which, alas, camouflaged the brain of an obstinate mule.

"Delphinium," she hissed, "it is not seemly to stare so at a gentleman."

Delphie tossed her curls. The effect, taken together with a saucy bonnet tied under her chin with ribbons, was adorable. Lady Burgess stifled a sigh.

If only the girl were more like dear Patricia. Patricia, though inexplicably fond of unladylike pursuits such as riding to hounds, was a sensible miss. Unfortunately at twenty-two she was also definitely old cattish. She spent too little time with her toilette and did not make the most of her looks. Her amber silk the other night had not been exceptional and today—

Lady Burgess clicked her tongue at Patricia's dove-gray vertical gown. Its close-fitting long sleeves and muslin neck ruff were too simple for her taste. As was her bonnet—*No town bronze and no sense of style,* Lady Burgess thought. But, at least, dear Patricia was a perfect foil for Delphinium's radiant beauty.

Delphinium was almost eighteen. This season would mark her London come-out. This was an expensive and exhausting undertaking, and the arrangements had taken the entire winter. But, Lady Burgess reflected, her daughter's penchant for falling in love with the wrong gentlemen could still ruin her chances for a good match.

It might be well, her ladyship thought shrewdly, if Delphinium learned what it was like to be attended by *eligible* gentlemen instead of by such fribble as dancing masters, curates, and poets. Lord Longe would be perfect in this regard, and so would Colonel Waldo Charteris.

"Yes," Lady Burgess murmured, "that will be most pleasant, indeed."

Patricia mistook her aunt's meaning. "Riverway *is* lovely, is it not? It reminds me of our home in Somerset."

Lovingly she thought of that childhood home where lately she had nursed Jack back to health. It was not overlarge, but very pretty with woods of ash and oak, an apple orchard, and the trout stream nearby. "Look," she exclaimed, "there is an apiary. They keep bees here, as we do in Somerset."

Freddy interrupted her, eagerly pointing out that there was a riding track beyond the apiary. "And s-someone's riding."

"It is Lord Longe," Patricia said.

Even at this distance she couldn't mistake those broad shoulders. With admiration she noted how easily he sat his bay stallion, and when he cleared a high hedge, she clapped her hands. "Bravo," she cried. "Well done."

As though he had heard her, his lordship slowed his mount and turned to look at them. The next moment he was riding toward them.

"Welcome," he exclaimed, "to Riverway Place."

Lord Longe's eyes sought Patricia's with such pleasure that she had the idiotish notion that his words were meant only for her. But there was no time to refine upon this as Lady Burgess had begun to gush.

"Then we are not *de trop*? We had *so* feared to inconvenience you, dear Lord Longe, but after all, since we *are* neighbors, we thought you would not mind."

Lord Longe made a polite response and tried not to show his distaste of the fruity perfume that emanated from the baronet.

"It's the neighborly thing to do, hey?" Lord Burgess was saying. He lowered his voice to a loud whisper and added, "Sorry about Farell, Longe. Fact is, the bleater met us on the road and insisted on coming with us. Damned nuisance, but couldn't very well fob him off."

The captain flushed. Delphie sent her father a killing look. Patricia saw amusement in Lord Longe's eyes as he nodded to the young officer.

"To what do I owe the pleasure, Captain?" Very stiffly the captain declared that he was there on business. "Perhaps it can keep until after we have had refreshments. If you will follow me?"

He cantered away up the broad path to the house and Freddy leaned over to whisper, "G-good thing you was with us, Pat. Lord Longe c-could have wished the rest of us in J-Jericho, but he brightened up when he s-saw *you!*"

"That is fudge." But Patricia's cheeks felt warm as the carriage followed horse and rider into a courtyard near a large stable and carriage house. Here grooms hurried to attend the horses, and a footman raced down the front steps to let down the step of the carriage. His lordship alighted and walked quickly over to hand the ladies down.

"Something like it, hey?" Lord Burgess exclaimed. He looked about him appreciatively, then sauntered up the stairs with his wife and daughter. Captain Farell followed them closely, and Lord Longe fell into step beside Patricia and Freddy.

"I'm glad you're here, Harmon," he said cordially. "There's a Welsh-bred gray that I want you to look over. Perhaps you'll give me your opinion."

Patricia waited for Freddy to stammer his thanks. She then added, "I would like to see that gray, too. I am rather fond of riding."

Mischief brightened Lord Longe's eyes. "Really, ma'am? I would not have guessed it in such a delicate lady."

"D-don't be fooled by her size," Freddy interposed loyally. "Pat's a c-clipping good rider. What's more, she c-can drive the pater's phaeton slap up on the echo, and you should s-see her ride to hounds."

"But surely you do not *hunt*, Miss Surrey? I cannot picture you riding neck-or-nothing over the field, braving ditch and hedge—and mud."

"Especially mud," Patricia agreed. Her face was sober but her eyes danced, and watching them, Lord Longe was reminded of sunlight glinting against autumn leaves.

So intent was he on Patricia that he nearly walked into the front door—a narrow miss that earned him an astonished look from the liveried footman who was standing there. Quelling this imprudent underling with a glare, the duke's son said, "As you can see, Riverway is quite rustic."

But this was hardly true, Patricia thought. The old house had been built out of golden Cottswold limestone and decorated for pleasure and comfort. Flowers, plants, and well-chosen statuary decorated the ground floor anteroom, and the oaken staircase that led to the first floor gleamed like silk. On this floor was a richly paneled room decorated in shades of rose and cream.

"How charming it all is, my lord," Lady Burgess effused. "I have quite lost my heart to Riverway. It is so elegant, yet so comfortable."

But, Patricia noted, one person did not look at all comfortable. In fact, Captain Farell's behavior was puzzling. Though he obviously could not keep his eyes off Delphie, he had placed himself as far as possible from her and was standing rigidly at attention near the door. It was almost as though he were on guard duty.

He remained at his post as, under the eye of a dignified butler, servants now served tea, cakes, confitures, and delicate sandwiches. As the company helped themselves to tea from bone-china cups, Lord Burgess cleared his throat confidentially.

"Hear you keep a remarkable set of cattle, Longe. I know something about horses myself." He popped several sandwiches in his mouth, masticated, then added rather indistinctly, "I aught to—been riding 'em and betting on 'em for years."

"L-lord Longe says he has a new Welsh g-gray," Freddy began eagerly.

He looked hopefully at his host, who said, "I thought Harmon might enjoy looking it over."

Lord Burgess crowed with laughter. "Waste of time, sir, waste of time. Freddy don't know about horses. He ain't a rider, nor a whipster neither. Not much of anything, come to think on't."

"Freddy," Lady Burgess broke in indignantly, "is delicate. You cannot imagine, dear Lord Longe, how a mother must suffer when her child's constitution is not *robust*."

The baronet swallowed another handful of sandwiches and growled, "Trouble with women is that they coddle their sons. No wonder the boy's a sallow, muffin-faced little bleater."

Lady Burgess looked wounded. Patricia bit her lips to prevent herself from protesting. Even Delphie, who had been surreptitiously trying to coax the captain further into the room, shot her brother a look of sympathy.

Lord Longe poured oil on the troubled waters. "You must hunt a great deal, Burgess. I've heard your pack in full cry."

Gratified, Lord Burgess announced that though he didn't pretend to be up to riding with the Quorn, he maintained a sizeable stable. "Good hounds, too. I hope you'll join us when we next ride to hounds, Longe, hey? There's an old dog fox, a cagey Reynard, I mean to catch."

He launched into a long hunting story. While pretending to listen, Lord Longe watched Patricia. As usual, she was dressed simply, and as usual, her unaffected elegance enhanced her loveliness. When her rueful eyes met his, his lordship wished that her impossible family would fly off to Hades so that he could be alone with her.

A movement from the door drew his attention to the ramrod-stiff captain. It was plain as a pikestaff that the young fool was smitten by the Harmon girl and had followed her to Riverway. But if this were the case, why did he look as though he'd swallowed castor oil?

Meanwhile the Burgesses were becoming tiresome. Lord Longe waited until there was a break in the baronet's monologue, then rose to his feet. "Your stable sounds several cuts above mine, but perhaps you'd like to look over my animals?" He put a hand on Freddy's shoulder adding, "Harmon and Miss Surrey have expressed a wish to see the Welsh gray."

Freddy was on his feet like a shot. Something in his host's steady look forestalled any comment from Lord Burgess. His lady struggled between a natural inclination to bid Freddy remain inside the house with her and a desire to please the duke's son.

She compromised by announcing, "I, also shall go to see the horses." Then, casting a withering eye on Captain Farell, she added firmly, "As will you, Delphinium."

But when she desired Freddy to muffle himself in his heavy cape, his scarf, and his hat, her son actually found the courage to refuse. "I'll not make a c-cake of myself by wearing all that, M-Mama."

"It is quite warm," Lord Longe added.

Though plainly annoyed, Lady Burgess held her peace. The ladies followed the gentlemen out into the sunlight and toward the riding track where grooms were walking several fine animals.

Lord Burgess whistled, "What magnificent cattle! A man could easily pay down six hundred guineas for one of these animals. If ever you decide to put some of your stud under the hammer, Longe," he added confidentially, "I'd be obliged to know about it."

He moved in to peer, pat, and inspect a roan stallion, but a gray horse caught Patricia's eye. "What a beauty," she exclaimed.

"His name is Caradoc, and he thanks you for your good opinion."

Lord Longe took the horse's bridle and led him forward. As Freddy began to stroke the gray's soft muzzle, Patricia heard the duke's son say softly, "I cannot tell you how pleased I am that you are here."

"I am glad of it," she replied in the same low tone. "Freddy was afraid that you might not welcome an invasion."

His eyes smiled in the way she well remembered. "Nonsense. Besides, I'd planned to ride to Burgess Hall tomorrow. Would I have been welcomed there, I wonder?"

Patricia chuckled. " 'Welcome' is too pale a word. Aunt and Uncle would have fallen on your neck, and as for Freddy—well, you must know that you are his champion."

"And would my visit have been welcome to you?"

She glanced swiftly up at him and then as quickly looked away. There was an intensity about him that was both exciting and disconcerting. With some effort Patricia managed an easy tone. "Of course it should. Why not?"

At that moment Freddy's excited voice intruded. "I s-say, Lord Longe, Caradoc's as trim as a trencher. I've never seen such a b-bang up set of b-blood and b-bone."

"I wish," Lady Burgess said acidly, "that you would not use cant expressions." She added, "Now that you have seen the horse my son, it is time to return to the house."

But Lord Longe intervened. "I thought you might enjoy putting Caradoc through his paces, Harmon. He's a sweet-tempered fellow, easy to handle."

Freddy looked as though heaven itself had opened before him. Patricia saw her uncle open his mouth to deliver one of his nasty set-downs and spoke quickly. "I am sure Freddy would like that above all things."

Her cousin shot her a glance of purest gratitude, but her aunt rounded on her. "Patricia, how can you? You know his delicate constitution. My lord," she continued earnestly, "I know that you are well meaning, but pray do not consider such a thing. Freddy must not expose himself to such a—to such danger."

"No danger, ma'am. I myself will ride beside Harmon at all times." Lord Longe draped an arm around Freddy's shoulders and added cheerfully, "Come walk with me, youngster, while the horses are being saddled."

As he drew Freddy out of his parents' line of fire, Lord Burgess chuckled. "Freddy on a horse. It'll be as good as watching a play."

His lady whirled upon him. "Hector!"

He looked somewhat alarmed. "Hey? What's that, m'dear?"

"*You* will also ride with Freddy, Hector." As the baronet began to protest, Lady Burgess added coldly, "Remember that you *laughed* at a mother's anxiety. If Freddy should come to harm, I shall not forgive you!"

"Oh, for God's sake, Maria!" But his lady was waving to the groom who was walking her husband's horse. "Was ever a man plagued by such a family of sapskulls?" Lord Burgess grumbled. "Longe's bound to think all of us are queerer than Dick's hatband."

Lord Longe's stallion and the Welsh gray were now led forward and with a groom's assistance, Freddy mounted the gray. Transfixed by his wife's quelling glare, Lord Burgess also clambered into the saddle.

They started at a decorous trot, but as they circled the riding track, the pace intensified. Lady Burgess held a hand to her heart.

"Dear heaven, they are *cantering*. And Burgess is not following them—he is falling back. Oh what can he be thinking of? Where are my salts? I feel faint."

Suddenly Lord Burgess uttered a yell. He bobbled about in the saddle for a few moments and then, with another shout, galloped across the riding track.

"He is riding straight for the river!"

As Patricia cried out, she saw her uncle's horse reach the riverbank. He bellowed something, toppled out of the saddle, and fell headlong into the water.

Lady Burgess began to scream. She lifted her skirts in both hands and, still screaming, ran toward the river. Delphie hurried after her. As Patricia was about to follow, she found that someone had caught her by the arm and was holding her back.

"Miss Surrey," Captain Farell said, "I must speak with you."

So silent had the Captain been that Patricia had almost forgotten he was there. She stared at him in astonishment. *"Now?"*

The captain lowered his voice. "Assure you— matter of utmost delicacy."

Patricia cast a distracted eye on the scene by the river. Lord Longe and Freddy were hauling her uncle out of the water while Delphie watched helplessly and the lamenting Lady Burgess wrung her hands.

"You must know that I am not the one to approach if you wish to discuss my cousin," she said distractedly. "Really, captain, I *must* go to my aunt."

The captain did not loosen his hold on her arm. "Not about Miss Harmon. Mean to say—concerns Lord Longe."

Patricia frowned. "I do not understand."

"I find it hard to begin."

"For heaven's sake," Patricia exclaimed impatiently. "Either say what you must or allow me to go and assist my aunt."

"Believe me—do not wish to be the bearer of bad tidings." Captain Farell let go of Patricia's arm and ran an agitated hand through his dark locks. "Colonel Charteris confided some matters to me that— may I speak frankly?"

"If only you would!"

"Lord Longe," said Captain Farell, "isn't the man he pretends to be."

She stared at him in bewilderment. "You mean that he is not the Duke of Parton's son?"

"Oh, that he is," the captain said. Bitterness tinged his voice as he added, "Noblesse oblige. Man must have a title or a fortune, or nothing is possible."

Patricia began to walk along the track. The captain hurried after her.

"Need to talk about Talavera," he said urgently. "Terrible battle—Colonel Charteris's aide killed— your brother wounded, Miss Surrey—much of the Nineteenth Foot Guard destroyed—all on account of the craven officer who lost his nerve and ordered his men to retreat."

"I know all this," Patricia began, but he cut her short.

"Lord Longe is that coward."

47

The world suddenly seemed to go very still. It was as though her heart itself had stopped. Then—"I do not believe you," Patricia cried.

Indignantly she rounded him. "If these accusations are true, why do you not confront Lord Longe? Why do you not allow him to defend himself instead of whispering slander behind his back?"

"Beg you to listen, ma'am!"

"I have listened to too much already," Patricia flared. "I tell you to your head that I do not believe you. You are either a malicious cad or you have been deceived by Colonel Charteris—which means that he is a liar."

Captain Farell flushed. "Why should he lie?"

"I collect that he took a dislike of Lord Longe the night of my aunt's rout and that this is his petty revenge." Patricia clenched her hands. "I should like to box his ears!"

Looking somewhat alarmed, the captain retreated several steps. "Assure you," he bleated, "truth—all of it. But Colonel Charteris's lips are sealed—Duke of Parton a powerful man."

"Which is to say that the colonel is afraid of being taken to court for slander," Patricia retorted scornfully. "So should I be if I told such a pack of lies."

Farell's agitation increased, and his speech became even more disjointed. "Should not have spoken, perhaps—was told all in strict confidence—should have held my tongue—could not. You consider Lord Longe a friend—honored guest at Burgess Hall—couldn't bear to see Miss Harmon—and her family—been taken in by a bad man like Lord Longshanks, don't you know."

"If anyone is being taken in, sir, it is you. I tell you—*what* did you call him just now?"

"Lord Longshanks. Name was given to him at Talavera, and it stuck—long legs carried him to safety while others died, you see." The young officer paused then added wrathfully. "No wonder the fellow doesn't like listening to talk about the war."

Patricia drew a deep breath. "I am going to repeat everything you said to Lord Longe. If he shoots both you and the colonel, I shall not blame him."

Without waiting for an answer, she began to hurry across the riding track. While she had been speaking with the captain, the rescue had been completed, and the others were returning from the river. Lord Burgess, wrapped in his host's coat, was dripping and complaining bitterly. Lady Burgess and Delphinium walked on either side of him, and Freddy followed leading the two horses.

And Lord Longe was riding toward her. Patricia stopped where she was and looked at him. "Impossible," she breathed.

He came up to her, dismounted, and smiled down at her. "Don't be alarmed, Miss Surrey, your uncle's unharmed," he said. "It seems the, er, perfume he wore attracted a bee."

"A bee! In February?"

His lordship shrugged.

"Perhaps this mild weather woke it before its time, and it was hungry. The bee stung Lord Burgess's horse, and the animal bolted." In spite of himself his lips quivered. "I'm going ahead to instruct my servants to prepare a hot bath for him."

Still, Patricia did not speak. In an altered voice he exclaimed, "You're very pale. Is something the matter?"

Patricia examined his frank, open face. She searched those clear eyes.

Impossible.

"I have heard something distressing," she told him. "Something so vile and insulting that I hardly dare repeat it."

His face hardened. "Who has dared to insult you?"

"The insult was to you, not me. Captain Farell says that Colonel Charteris told him that—that you are Lord Longshanks."

There was a small ripple of wind. It blew between them carrying the scent of new-mown hay and the sound of Lord Burgess's carping voice. For a moment this was all. And then, incredibly, Lord Longe laughed.

"Is that all?"

"*All?* But surely you know what that implies." He was silent and she cried, "It is criminal to repeat such slander, and so I told that captain. I would not blame you if you horsewhipped Colonel Charteris."

She broke off in the face of his rueful smile. "Well," he said, "I'd have to horsewhip at least a hundred men. I own that I was never fond of that nickname, but it stuck to me like a burr."

She couldn't believe that he was saying these things. She faltered, "But you cannot be—"

Faint surprise filled the gray eyes. "Lord Longshanks? Alas, I am. But other officers had worse nicknames, believe me."

She had turned so pale that he was afraid she would faint. He put out a hand to steady her, but she shrank back from him as though he were unclean.

"Then *you* were the officer in charge? *You* ordered the Nineteenth Foot Guard to retreat?"

Lord Longe's dark brows drew together in a puzzled frown. "Yes. Why do you ask?"

It was true. The whole, filthy story that Colonel Charteris had told was the truth. Patricia stared hard at Lord Longe and saw not that healthy, hard-planed face but her brother's pale countenance.

"You beastly cad," she cried, and slapped him.

All the force of her arm was in that blow. The impact of it stung Patricia's hand. The hurt traveled all the way up her arm and shoulder till it reached her heart.

"It is your fault that Jack was wounded."

She wanted to slap him again, but he caught her hand and held it fast. He had gone very white except for the mark on his cheek. "What did you say?" he gritted.

She wanted to shout out his perfidy, but her words came out in a hating gasp. "Because of you the Nineteenth Foot Guard were cut down at Talavera. Because of your cowardice. Their blood is on your head, Lord Longe."

Next moment she cried out, for his grip tightened. "Is that what Farell told you?" She did not need to reply—the blaze of hatred in her eyes was answer enough. "And you believed him!"

Something grim and bitter in his deep voice reached her, and she was filled with sudden doubt. And hope. Could a man sound like that, *look* like that, if he were guilty?

"You deny it?"

Lord Longe was much too angry to hear the hope in Patricia's voice. He could not believe that she had been taken in by Farell's lies and had condemned him out of hand. Behind the cool mask he wore, he was seething. In that moment he almost hated Patricia Surrey.

He dropped his hold on her and said, "If *you* believe what Farell said, it must be true."

Patricia was confused and angry. She did not hear the pain struggling with the lashed-raw pride in his voice. She had trusted this man. She had thought him kind and decent. She had laughed with him and told him about her childhood and of her love for Jack. The memory of his strong arms around her and of his cool lips on her hand sickened her.

"I wish," Patricia whispered, "that I were a man. I would call you out and shoot you."

His laugh was harsh. "I'm accounted a very good shot. I doubt if you'd succeed."

Patricia felt as though a vice had been clamped about her head. She felt physically ill, but she would not let herself be sick in front of *him*.

Contempt blazed in her eyes. "You believe that nothing can touch you because you are a duke's son. But to me you are worse than the lowest vermin. I hate you and despise you, 'Lord Longshanks,' " she added passionately, "and I will never forgive you."

Chapter Four

A blackbird was singing in a copse of young ash trees, and the sparrows were busy with their breakfast when Mr. Percival Yancey, splendorous in pale yellow breeches, white-topped riding boots, and a redingote with stiffly padded shoulders, drove his curricle up to Riverway Place. He tossed his reins to a nearby groom, alighted, and shivered languidly.

"Bedad if it ain't colder than charity. Hulloa, Andrews," he added to the dignified individual who had appeared at the front door. "Your master still at breakfast?"

"No, Mr. Yancey. In point of fact, sir, his lordship is not at home."

Astonished, Mr. Yancey surveyed his friend's valet through his quizzing glass. Andrews had followed his master to the wars and had endured marches, bivouacs, and battles without so much as breaking into a sweat. Yet this morning Andrews looked worried.

"Hunting, is he?" Mr. Yancey conjectured.

"Riding, sir."

Under the scrutiny of one of his lordship's oldest friends, Andrews almost but not quite permitted himself a sigh. He had been in Lord Longe's employ for near on fifteen years, and he had never seen his lordship in such a taking. As soon as Lord Burgess and his family had departed last evening, he had roared for his horse and ridden off as if the devil himself were at his back. He had not returned until midnight, at which time he had abruptly dismissed his valet. "I don't need you, Andrews—go to bed," he had snapped.

What had caused his usually even tempered lordship to look so black and fly up into the boughs? The servants speculated in hushed voices belowstairs without finding an answer, and Andrews owned himself truly worried. His lordship had looked like this only once before, and that day was too terrible to remember.

This morning, Lord Longe had risen before dawn. From his looks he hadn't slept all night, but he had refused both assistance and breakfast and instead had gone striding off to the stables. Moments later he was on Sultan's back and thundering off to God alone knew where.

"Wonder what the deuce has got into the fellow, racketing about at this time of day," Mr. Yancey was musing.

As he spoke, hoofbeats sounded in the far distance. Andrews stiffened like a hound on the scent, and the head groom came racing out of the stables to look down the road.

"There come t'master," he shouted.

A few moments later, a rider on a lathered stallion came galloping down the road. Mr. Yancey commenced to stroll toward the stable and arrived in time to hear his lordship say, "I'll see to Sultan myself, Heeming."

The groom protested, "But think on, master, tha has not had thy breakfast."

Lord Longe said nothing, but there was a steely flash in his eyes. As the groom hurriedly took himself off, Mr. Yancey wondered what had pissed his friend's goose.

"Hulloa, Jonathan," he called.

Lord Longe looked up, and the hard look in his eyes was replaced by astonishment. "Percival," he exclaimed. "I thought you were in London."

"Well, I ain't. You aught to know I was coming down—I wrote you a wafer, didn't I?" When Lord Longe told him he had done no such thing, Mr. Yancey rubbed his comfortable chin. "Thought I did. Wanted to tell you that I bought two of Vetter's breakdowns before they came to market. Deuced good pair they are, too. Wanted you to try them out with me this morning, Jonathan."

"If you'll wait till I've seen to Sultan, I'll oblige you," Lord Longe began to walk his stallion around the riding track adding, as his friend fell into step beside him, "What are you doing in Sussex? I thought you hated the country."

"Mother's got some maggoty idea that all of us should be under one roof for Father's birthday—not that the old gentleman cares. *He's* happy with country pleasures." Mr. Yancey heaved a deep sigh. "Pleasures, bedad. Last night we were guests of some new neighbor—I forget his name—and sat down to cards with the worst bores I ever met in m'life. Lucky, bores, too. That jackass Burgess pocketed most of the ready, but our host didn't fare badly neither. Now *what* the deuce was his name? Charteris."

Lord Longe rapped out a word that made his friend clap his quizzing glass to his eye. "What has got you into such a pucker?" he wondered.

His lordship made no reply. Yesterday, after *she* had gone, he had ridden for miles, for hours, but neither the rolling downs or the raging pace he'd set for himself had exorcised the memory of how Patricia Surrey had looked at him.

I will never forgive you, she had said. *I despise you, Lord Longshanks.*

"Damnation," he swore.

Sultan whickered sympathetically and gently nibbled at his shoulder. It was as though the horse knew what his master was feeling.

Lord Longe wasn't sure *what* he felt. Yesterday he had been so furious that as soon as he reached Riverway, he'd gone in search of Farell. He'd intended to thrash an explanation out of the man before sending Charteris his cartel, but unfortunately the captain had already left Riverway.

Left with his unwelcome guests, Lord Longe had maintained an icy courtesy. Later, when the baronet had borrowed dry clothing and was on the point of departure, he had even wished Patricia Surrey a good journey home. The only answer she'd given him was a glance so filled with loathing that he had itched to strangle her. Instead, he'd shouted for his horse.

"I must have been mad," Lord Longe muttered.

"Don't know about that, old boy," Mr. Yancey

replied judiciously. " 'Struth that I haven't seen you look so black since we was at Eton together and Old Culpepper thrashed you for something you hadn't done. Unjust of the old squeeze-crab. Served him damned well right when you popped that bat into his wig during chapel." Mr. Yancey began to swing his quizzing glass to and fro as he added, "Something's nicked you on the raw, Long Johnny, and you can't scratch it."

Hearing his old school nickname made Lord Longe smile. Then the smile disappeared. "Percival, I've just had a reminder of Talavera."

As he sketched the scene with Patricia Surrey, Mr. Yancey's eyes widened. "Oh, bedad," he exclaimed. "It's a wonder you didn't strangle this Surrey female."

"I came near to it." But his lordship spoke calmly, for the madness was gone. Instead of rage, all he now felt was pain. *How could she think it of me?* he wondered.

Mr. Yancey was saying, "Now that I think on it, Charteris mentioned Talavera last night during cards. Didn't catch much of it at first—half asleep through the whole ghastly evening, give you m'word—but Father brought him up sharpish. Said you was like a member of the family." He gave his quizzing glass another spin. "Charteris held his tongue after that, but I shouldn't wonder if he's spreading his slum elsewhere. You should have told the Surrey female the facts, Jonathan."

With a shrewdness that belied his plump, placid countenance, Mr. Yancey enumerated the known facts. The Nineteenth Foot Guards had sailed to Lisbon with Colonel Sir Arthur Wellesley, helped him rout the French Soult, then faced Marshal Victor at Talavera. During this battle, the Nineteenth had been all but decimated by a horrendous cannonade. Major Lord Jonathan Longe's superior officer had been killed almost immediately along with fully half of his men.

"The cannons was murdering you as you stood," Mr. Yancey continued. "Then Boney's cuirassiers charged you. Naturally, as ranking officer, you ordered a retreat to a better position. There you reestablished battle formation and repulsed the frogs."

Following Talavera, Lord Longe had requested an official Board of Inquiry in London. He had much to say to the board, but though it had exonerated him and even commended him for gallantry, it had not listened to his theory that the cannons that cut down the Nineteenth Foot Guard could not possibly have been French.

Lord Longe thought of his dying men. He remembered the battlefield smoke, the incessant crack of musket fire, and the cannonade that came from a position where no enemy cannon could be. If he had told Patricia Surrey what he suspected, would she have believed him? He doubted it.

He said to Mr. Yancey, "After the battle there was a rumor that I'd cut and run, thus causing my panicked men to blunder into French fire. I don't know where the rumor started, and no one who knew me believed it for a moment. Why is Charteris repeating it now?"

"Bedad, I'll act as your second. In fact," Mr. Yancey added with uncharacteristic energy, "I'll carry your cartel to Charteris on the way home. "Twould be a pleasure to watch you shoot that pompous windbag."

Lord Longe put a hand on his friend's shoulder. "I'm not going to call him out."

"Eh?"

"Much as I'd enjoy putting a bullet through Charteris, it won't stop the talk. Nor will Charteris's death convince Miss Surrey."

Mr. Yancey's eyes became shrewd again. "What is she like, this Surrey female?"

Hair as rich as honey, hazel eyes that could sparkle with sunlight and laughter—Lord Longe thought of holding a slender, rose-scented woman in his arms and felt an ache of loss that was almost physically painful.

I despise you, Lord Longshanks, and I will never, never forgive you.

He turned away to hide his anguish. "I can't blame her, Percival. Her brother is all she has in the world, and he was nearly killed at Talavera."

"But if you told her the truth—"

"I don't *know* the damned truth," his lordship exploded. "Those French cannons *could* not have been there, and yet they butchered us." He paused to add in a quieter tone, "Percival, I don't understand it myself. How can I possibly explain what happened at Talavera to Miss Surrey?"

"What's happened is that I'm up the River Tick," Lord Burgess gloomed.

He glared at his wife, who wondered, "Shall I use the crimson or the pale pink for the roses? I favor crimson, but Lady Burnes informed me the other day that pink roses are quite the fashion in London. Patricia, my dear, what do you think?"

Seated by the window of the morning room, her eyes fixed on the garden below, Patricia did not even hear her aunt. A heavy rain had blown up and water fairly sluiced down the eaves of Burgess Hall. Raindrops beat down the hopeful snowdrops, drowned the rosebushes, and thickly beaded the French windows that reflected Patricia's pale face.

Since returning from Riverway Place, her cheeks had lost their bloom. Patricia moved with a brittle, almost feverish energy, and sometimes she fell into uneasy silences. Her thoughts wandered. Today, unable to sit idly, she had brought some handkerchiefs to hem, but the cambric squares lay untouched in a basket by her feet.

"Crimson or pink, Patricia?" Lady Burgess repeated. "I am persuaded that you are rainbow-chasing, my dear."

"You have been doing that often of late," Delphie suggested mischievously. "Also you are looking pale and wan, which is a telltale sign in all the books I have read. I collect that you are pining for a certain dark-haired gentleman."

Patricia shuddered violently. "You are wrong," she cried.

Freddy looked up from the book he was reading, and Delphie exclaimed, "Why fly up into the boughs? I thought you and Lord Longe were friends."

Lord Burgess picked up on the word. "Friends, forsooth," he snorted. "It's all your fault, Maria. If you hadn't been so anxious to have that fellow at your rout, we'd not be in this mare's nest."

"What m-mare's nest are you talking about, sir?" Freddy wondered.

Ignoring his son, the baronet addressed his wife sarcastically. "How do we deal with a man who's showed the white feather at Talavera? Hey? Your books of etiquette should tell you the answer to that one, Maria."

Lady Burgess looked astonished. "Surely, Hector, you are mistaken. You are speaking of a duke's son."

"Who s-said that Lord Longe is a coward?" Freddy asked indignantly.

"I had it from Colonel Charteris. He said something when we sat down to cards the other night, but Yancey stopped him. Yesterday, he told me the whole sorry story."

Freddy sprang up from his chair. "I d-don't believe it," he cried. "Lord Longe isn't that k-kind of man."

"Anyone who thinks *you* capable of riding a horse is a fool," his loving father retorted. "So why shouldn't he be a loose screw as well, hey? There's even a ditty they sang about Longe at Talavera."

He commenced to sing in an unmusical tenor:

> They shout it high,
> They shout it low,
> They shout it far and near-o.
> Curses on Lord Longshanks,
> The coward of Talaver-o.

Lord Burgess looked about him to see what effect his song had had. Freddy looked furious, Delphie bewildered, and Patricia had gone very pale. Lady Burgess put a hand to her heart and quietly fainted.

"Good God," Lord Burgess shouted. "Maria—hey, Maria!"

Freddy attempted to reach his mother's side, fell over an occasional table, and upset a lamp that knocked over the fire tongs. Lord Burgess insisted that everyone should be calm. Patricia hurried to her aunt's side, loosed her stays, and bade Delphie fetch her mother's smelling salts. Delphie left the morning room at a run and almost immediately returned with the salts and Miss Wigge.

"*Dear* Lady Burgess," the governess twittered. "How came this to pass? Evil news from abroad—from poor Mr. Harmon, perchance? Alas, 'when sorrows come, they come not single spies but in battalions.' "

"Nothing's wrong with Lionel," Lord Burgess growled. "So don't put ideas into her head."

Miss Wigge chafed Lady Burgess's wrists, begged her to be of good heart, and followed with several disjointed quotations. Under cover of this noise Freddy sidled over to Patricia.

"The p-pater's dicked in the nob," he whispered. "To think that a m-man like Lord Longe c-could be cow-hearted—I never heard such s-slum."

There was a burning ache behind Patricia's eyes, and she could not rid herself of it. As she had done many times since leaving Riverway, she wished that she had never seen or heard of Lord Longe.

Freddy was continuing, "Maybe Lord Longe s-said something about d-disliking war, and the colonel misinterpreted everything. Pompous ass. I d-don't believe he knows any of the generals—or Sir Arthur Wellesley neither."

He was interrupted by a wail from Lady Burgess. "Hector, do you stand there and tell me that the Duke of Parton's son is a coward?"

"The coward of Talavera." Satisfied at the commotion he had caused, Lord Burgess puffed out a chest encased in a handsome smoking jacket of maroon velvet. "I'm not one to wrap plain facts in clean linen, Maria."

"But—but this is hideous beyond belief," Lady Burgess moaned. "Everybody knows that we have received him at Burgess Hall. I have begged him to call upon us whenever he pleases. You have invited him to hunt with you."

Lord Burgess frowned, "I'll cancel the invitation."

"You cannot do that. His father is the Duke of Parton."

" 'Oh, put not your trust in princes,' " Miss Wigge quoted helpfully, " 'for there is no help in them.' "

Directing a quelling look at the governess, Lord Burgess said that he didn't care whether the fellow was in line for the throne of England.

"He's not setting foot in my house," he added. "Hey? I told Charteris he could count on us—but that's another story."

He winked at his wife and sent a significant look in the direction of his daughter, who looked back in bewilderment and asked, "Whatever can you mean, Papa?"

Lord Burgess chuckled richly. "You slyboots, do you sit there and tell me that you don't know when you've caught a gentleman's eye?" Delphie blushed and dimpled. "He asked me last night whether I'd permit him to call on you, and I agreed that he might."

Delphie jumped up from her chair, ran to her father and threw her arms around his neck. "Oh, Papa!" she cried. Then, struck by a new thought she added, "But what does Mama say?"

Distracted momentarily from her visions of social ruin, Lady Burgess exclaimed, "What should I say, pray? Colonel Charteris is a most eligible suitor. There is the connection to Teglare. There is also fifteen thousand pounds a year, and property in London, Sussex, Devon, and—"

She was interrupted by a wail from Delphie, who dropped her arms from about her father's neck and retreated several steps. "Colonel *Charteris*? But I thought you meant—"

She broke off and caught a rosy underlip between her teeth. Her father warned, "We've got to be careful about the company we keep. Hey? We've got our good name to think about and our position in the county. I thanked Charteris for warning me about that loose fish, Longe. Forewarned is forearmed."

"Well if that ain't the m-most ramshackle b-business," Freddy exploded. Then, sustaining a withering look from his parent, he began to wilt. "P-Pat," he hissed. "*You* t-tell them."

Patricia remained as mute as stone. It was her aunt who lamented, "But it will not *do*. If we insult the son, we insult the father. His Grace of Parton is much respected and feared in the House of Lords. *Feared*, Hector."

From her place by the window Patricia watched her uncle's expression turn obstinate. "What can he do to us, hey?" he blustered. "This is England, not some heathenish country. I tell you, Maria, the fellow's not going to set foot in Burgess Hall."

There was a knock on the door and a discreet cough as Charms, the butler, glided in to announce a visitor. As he proffered a card on a silver tray to Lady Burgess, Freddy spoke in Patricia's ear. "I s-say, are you all right? You d-don't look the thing, if you know what I mean. In fact, you look s-sick—"

A shriek from Lady Burgess interrupted him. "Oh, Hector, we are undone."

"What's the matter now?"

Through pallid lips, Lady Burgess declaimed, "Lord Longe has come to call."

The news struck Patricia almost viscerally. How could *he* come to Burgess Hall after all she had said to him? He could not be here. There had to be some mistake.

"Tell him we're not in, Charms," Lord Burgess was ordering.

Charms bowed himself out. There was the sound of murmuring voices and then the noise of a door closing. Grateful beyond words that the hateful Lord Longshanks had departed, Patricia sank into the nearest chair.

"I'm gratified to see you looking so well," a deep voice said.

Lord Burgess swore aloud, but Patricia did not hear him. All her attention was riveted on the man who stood, smiling, in the doorway.

Far from having gone away, Lord Longshanks was here and very much at home. He looked as neat as wax in his double-breasted jacket with brass buttons. His cravat had been tied by a masterful hand, and his brocaded waistcoat was elegance itself as were the fawn breeches that disappeared into glossy riding boots.

"Lord Longe," Lady Burgess moaned.

Bowing as though nothing were amiss, the duke's son strolled into the cluttered room. His height, his breadth of shoulder, and his air of command seemed to dwarf them all. Gallantly he bowed over Lady Burgess's hand.

"Your most obedient servant, ma'am. I've been

remiss, I own. I'd meant to ride out before this, but there were one or two things I needed to settle at Riverway Place."

Lady Burgess could only manage a croak. The duke's son smiled at her kindly before turning to her crimson-faced spouse. "Glad to see that you've recovered from your wetting, Burgess."

He held out a hand as he spoke, and Patricia saw her uncle's jaws work. Lord Burgess wanted to cut the duke's son, but he lacked the courage to do so. Reluctantly he shook hands and mumbled a greeting.

Lord Longe now turned to Freddy. "And how are you, Harmon?"

Avoiding his father's eyes, Freddy spoke eagerly. "Th-thank you, sir, I'm v-very well indeed."

Like an abominable farce, the greetings continued. Delphie murmured a bewildered response, Miss Wigge twittered nervously, and now Lord Longe was saying, "I hope I find you well, Miss Surrey."

Patricia said nothing and let her eyes speak for her.

Lord Longe had seen eyes like hers over cold steel at twenty paces. Goaded by the hatred and contempt he saw reflected there, his own anger blazed up. But before he could give it full rein, Freddy asked, "I hope that Caradoc is well, s-sir?"

The boy's question recalled Lord Longe's common sense just in time. He even managed a smile. "He does very well, but he needs a proper rider. The grooms exercise him, of course, but that's seldom the same thing."

Though she very much misliked Freddy's championship of Lord Longshanks, Patricia had to admire her cousin's rare show of courage. Heedless of black looks from his father, Freddy continued, "I m-must thank you for letting me ride Caradoc, sir."

"I wish you'd do me the favor again."

There was a sound like rusty hinges in use—Lord Burgess was clearing his throat. "Any *particular* reason for your being here, Longe?" he wondered.

His tone was as rude as he dared make it, but the duke's son seemed impervious to insult. "No reason except the desire to see more of my favorite neighbors."

Patricia watched her uncle's plump cheeks darken to magenta. He looked about to speak, but again let discretion get the better part of valor and remained glumly silent as his lady offered refreshments.

Lord Longe took a seat beside Lady Burgess and smiled sunnily at them all. "How delightful it is to be among friends," he declared.

In a voice that she hardly recognized as her own, Patricia asked, "*Do* you have friends, my lord?"

One dark eyebrow slanted up. "Do I not, ma'am?" he countered.

"I do not think so." Patricia was aware of Freddy's incredulous gaze as she added recklessly, "You see, it is true that brave men are respected and loved. When brother lay near to death, many of his friends came to call. They would have grieved for him had he died. How many people would grieve for you?"

Lady Burgess looked frightened. Then, as footsteps approached the door, she added hopefully, "That will be the sherry."

As the morning room door swung open, Lord Longe leaned toward Patricia. "Ah, but there are friends and friends, Miss Surrey." She glared at him, and he added, "Anyone who had your goodwill would be rich indeed."

"That you shall never have," she cried. "Why have you come here?"

Before Lord Longe could answer, Charms announced that Captain Farell had come to call.

Delphie flushed, jumped to her feet, and then as quickly sat down again. Lord Burgess was gulping, "Is the colonel with him?"

But the captain was alone. He and a tray of ratafia and sherry arrived simultaneously a few moments later. The captain, his dark hair romantically slicked down by the rain, entered smiling, but the smile died as soon as he saw Lord Longe.

"Good God," he ejaculated. Then, contemptuously, he averted his eyes from the duke's son. *Well done, Captain,* Patricia applauded silently, but she saw that Farell's direct cut did not seem to trouble Lord Longe. If anything, he looked amused.

"My lord and lady," the captain announced, "I have a letter—charged by Colonel Charteris to deliver it to Miss Harmon, don't you know—Colonel's unwell."

He bent an ardent look on Delphie, then quickly averted his eyes. Very conscious of that look, Delphie fluttered her long lashes.

"I thank you, Captain," she exclaimed demurely. "How kind of you to bring me the colonel's letter."

Miss Wigge began a string of quotations. Lord Burgess seemed gratified for a moment, then looked uneasy. Farell was sure to squeak beef to the colonel and tell him that Lord Longe had been visiting Burgess Hall.

If the fellow would only leave—but he seemed immune to hints. At his noble ease he was sipping sherry and watching Delphie read the colonel's letter.

But it was not Delphie that Lord Longe was watching. Patricia, who had taken a seat beside her cousin, was conscious of his lordship's steady appraisal. She attempted to ignore him, but her mind was like a cat worrying a mouse. Why was he still here? she wondered. Captain Farell had cut him. Her uncle had been rude. Any man of sense would have left long before now.

Determinedly Patricia fixed her attention on her cousin, who was looking like a kitten who had swallowed a cream pot.

"It is too bad," she announced cheerfully. "*Poor* Colonel Charteris writes that he has contacted a chill and will be indisposed for some time."

Lady Burgess was at once alarmed. "It is the fault of this weather," she exclaimed. "Freddy, you are not dressed warmly enough. Move closer to the fire."

"Since he himself cannot come to Burgess Hall," Delphie continued blithely, "the colonel begs that you will allow him to send his compliments by Captain Farell. He hopes that the time will come soon when he can greet us in person once again."

Miss Wigge was moved to murmur that the course of true love seldom ran smooth. "Surely, dear Miss Harmon, the captain will carry your answer to the colonel?" she added.

Lord Burgess nodded approval, and his lady exclaimed, "Miss Wigge is right. Delphinium, my love, you must write a few lines to the dear colonel and inquire about his health."

Delphie rose to her feet and swayed gracefully toward the other end of the room. Here she paused beside a desk that had been crammed between a chest and a lacquered daybed.

"May I have your assistance, Captain Farell?" she wondered.

The young officer quivered as though he had sustained an electric shock. "Certainly—anything you like, ma'am—immediately," he stuttered. "Er—what can I do?"

Delphie looked demure. "The colonel mentions that his cold has been aggravated by an old wound he received in the war. Being a mere female, I know nothing about battles, and I do not wish to sound goosish. Can you help me find the correct words?"

Lady Burgess's brow puckered uncertainly as the captain joined Delphie at the desk. Then she forgot about her daughter and Farell. There was a far more serious problem at hand.

The problem was calmly discussing racing, curricles, and horses with Freddy. Lord Burgess, who had been listening moodily, caught his wife's worried glance and cleared his throat.

"Don't know why you stay on in the country, Longe," he began. "Thought you'd be back in London by now. Season's beginning soon, ain't it, hey?"

The words by themselves were not offensive—the tone was. But the duke's son merely shrugged. "There's much to be done at Riverway Place, and I have many friends in the area."

Patricia knew those words were for her benefit. She wished that the flames in the fireplace were the fires of hell and that Lord Longe was roasting in them.

"Besides," Lord Longe continued, "Sussex has many charms."

Patricia clenched her hands into tight fists. She would not, she swore to herself, look at *him* again or acknowledge him in any way. That was the only way to deal with someone like Lord Longe. Studiously ignoring him, she looked toward Delphie, who was saying, "Oh, Captain, you have found exactly the right word."

"Hey?" Lord Burgess demanded. "What right word?"

Smiling, Delphie sealed her letter and handed it to the captain in such a way that their hands clasped momentarily.

"Captain Farell is so clever," she dimpled. "He has shown me how to write 'good-bye' in Spanish."

"There are some who don't know how to say 'good-bye' in any language," Lord Burgess growled.

"A timely reminder that I mustn't wear out my welcome." Lord Longe bent over Lady Burgess's hand. "With your permission, ma'am, I will call again. Your son has expressed a desire to ride with me in my curricle."

Lady Burgess blanched. Lord Burgess shot a withering look at his son, but Freddy continued to defy parental displeasure. "I would l-like it above all things," he cried. "I will look forward to your v-visit, sir."

Lord Longe looked pleased with himself. His arrogance so infuriated Patricia that she forgot her vow to ignore him. In her clear voice she said, "Good-bye, Lord Longshanks."

The words were flung out like a challenge, and for a moment she had the satisfaction of knowing that she had angered him. His gray eyes narrowed, and his mouth tightened. Then he bowed to her.

"Until we meet again," he said—and smiled.

Goaded beyond her control, Patricia completely forgot herself. "Oh, hell and the devil," she cried, "I hope I may never set eyes on you again."

Miss Wigge gasped. Lady Burgess sank swooning back into her chair. Even Lord Burgess looked astounded.

Lord Longe's smile had widened into a grin. Patricia wished she had something to throw at him. But nothing was at hand. She could only glare impotently as he promised, "You'll see me soon, Miss Surrey. Very soon indeed."

Chapter Five

Patricia had seldom seen such a beautiful morning.

The March wind had gentled to a breeze, and the grass was showing green. Drops of dew clung like pearls to the primroses and early daffodils, officious robins hopped about the garden path, and a thrush sang blissfully from the high hawthorn hedge that bordered Lady Burgess's rose garden.

Delphie's voice and Miss Wigge's answering titter were coming from beyond this hedge. Patricia slowed her steps. She really was not in a mood for disjoined quotations, but—"It is my fault," she thought contritely. "I have the blue devils this morning."

The blue devils had begun over breakfast, during which Lord Burgess had castigated Freddy for his stubborn support of Lord Longe. "You're to have nothing to do with him in the future," the baronet had concluded. "Is that clear?"

A rebellious look had hardened Freddy's usually mild countenance. "I d-don't see why. L-lots of people think the world of L-Lord L-Longe. Lord and Lady Yancey, and their sons, for instance. Ain't that s-so, Mama?"

Looking harried, Lady Burgess was forced to agree. "I had it from Diana Sinclair that Lord Longe was a guest at Countess Bellingford's turtle supper. *We* were not invited to that event, if you recall." She paused and added anxiously, "I cannot but feel that it is unwise to be so outspoken against the Duke of Parton's son. *Noblesse oblige*, Hector."

"Must you be flinging plaguey Greek phrases at my head?" her spouse had retorted. "Longe might be received because of his father, but there's talk, depend on it. Many families hereabouts have lost men in the war, and they believe what Charteris says. I won't have my son being bosom-bows with the coward of Talavera."

Cowed into silence, Freddy had shot his cousin a bitter look. Thinking of that black glance now, Patricia felt saddened and lonely. Freddy's wrongminded championship of Lord Longe had caused a bitter rift.

A laugh from behind the hedge increased her loneliness, and she wished with all her heart that her brother were home. If Jack were here, they could ride afield, and she could tell him how she had been deceived into actually liking and trusting Lord Longe.

Suddenly an odd sound intruded into her thoughts. Unmusical notes were coming from the rose garden. It sounded, Patricia thought, as if a cat were sharpening its claws on a piece of slate.

Then, mercifully, the dissonance stopped. "Damn

it," Captain Farell's aggrieved voice exclaimed. "Hem! That is to say—beg you will excuse my language. This da—confounded thing is hard to master."

Patricia approached the tall hedge, stood on tiptoe, and peered into the rose garden. Here she saw Captain Farell frowning over a lute. And this was not all. Patricia noted that today the captain had put off his regimentals and was garbed in black knee breeches and a white, open-necked shirt with flowing sleeves. A red sash had been wound around his midriff. All he needed to look like a gypsy was a gold earring.

Delphie couldn't seem to take her eyes away from the romantic, if unconventional, figure the officer made. Seated on a marble bench, she herself looked extremely pretty with a lamb's wool shawl tucked picturesquely about her dress of pink-flocked muslin. Miss Wigge, muffled in a voluminous black cloak, was seated some distance away.

"Please, Captain, try the song again," Delphie begged prettily.

The young officer set his booted foot on the edge of Delphie's chair, lifted his instrument to his knee, and drew his fingers across the strings. A hideous noise resulted.

"Oh, hell—I mean, confound it," the captain exclaimed.

He struck another chord, and Patricia winced. Captain Farell, she decided, was either a total fool or a very courageous man.

He had certainly braved the wet February weather and the winds of March to act as Colonel Charteris's emissary. Cheerfully explaining that his chief was still suffering from the effects of his cold, the captain had carried letters and flowers and gifts daily to Burgess Hall. Earlier this week, he had brought roses in a crystal holder. Day before yesterday, the gift had been a basket heaped with grapes out of season. Today, here was the lute.

Once again the captain put his fingers to the strings. He managed to produce one or two tolerable notes and Miss Wigge clasped her thin hands to her chest. " 'If music be the food of love, play on,' " she quoted coyly. "How true it is that music can soothe even the most savage breast."

"Don't know about that, ma'am. Seems to me—anybody listening to this stuff would feel pretty savage. Stands to reason, don't you know." Captain Farell gave the strings an experimental twang. "Can't seem to get the hang of it."

Delphie protested, "But the lute is such a *romantic* instrument. Tristan played to Isolde on a lute. Blondel found Richard the Lion-Hearted through his lute."

"Heard about that," the captain exclaimed. "Minstrel fellow, wasn't he? Trailed around Palestine playing and singing—located the king in a dungeon—amazing thing. Should have thought he'd have been arrested as a public nuisance."

Patricia could not help laughing. She walked around the hedge and into the garden and greatly discomfited the captain, who nearly dropped his lute as he bowed to her.

Since their confrontation at Riverway, Captain Farell had taken care to stay out of Patricia's way. Patricia guessed that he felt that she blamed him for revealing that Lord Longe was the coward of Talavera. Now he stood regarding her so nervously that she took pity on him.

76

"Have you taken up lessons in music, Captain?" she asked.

It was Delphie who replied. "Captain Farell is *so* thoughtful, Patricia. Because I expressed a desire to hear a serenade on the lute, he has learned the instrument."

The captain cleared his throat. "Not *learned*, Miss Harmon—attempted—failed, I'm afraid. Soldier, not a minstrel—yours to command anyhow."

" 'Being your slave,' " Miss Wigge quoted, " 'what should I do but tend/ Upon the hours and times of your need?' "

Captain Farell became even redder and crushed his lute to his chest. The mistreated instrument popped two strings.

"Ah, dear Miss Surrey," fluted Miss Wigge, "you are choking. Can it be that you are catching cold? That would be most distressing."

"Bad thing, March colds," the captain agreed. "Look at the colonel—laid up with it for weeks." He added cheerfully, "And not likely to get any better soon, either."

He and Delphie exchanged such meaningful looks that Patricia wondered why Miss Wigge did not intervene. The governess, however, had her eyes tight shut and was murmuring a love sonnet from Shakespeare.

"Captain Farell—I mean, the colonel, of course—has even written me a poem," Delphie announced. "Would you like to hear it, Patricia?"

The captain immediately began to protest. "Rubbishy thing—not fit to be heard, don't you know. Play the lute instead."

He attempted to repair the strings while Delphie coaxed, "Please, Captain, do read the poem."

The captain looked desperate. "Becoming cold," he hedged. "Miss Surrey coughing—may catch cold—should return to the house."

Delphie pouted adorably.

With a heartfelt sigh the young officer laid down his lute and, producing a sheet of paper from the recesses of his voluminous shirt, began to read very rapidly:

Your eyes are like violets after the snow
Your lips are scarlet—they spell my woe.
Your slightest wish is command to me
Who am your slave for eternity.

"Hey? What's this 'slave' business?"

Lord Burgess's astounded face was barely visible over the top of the hawthorn hedge. Miss Wigge gave a little shriek, and the captain jerked to attention as the baronet trotted into the rose garden.

"Didn't hear you ride up, Farell," Lord Burgess said. "Why didn't you come up to the house instead of—" he broke off and frankly stared.

The captain attempted to pull the folds of his cloak about him. "Orders, sir," he exclaimed.

"You mean that *Charteris* had you dress up in that—that costume and sent you over here to serenade my daughter? No, you're bamming me."

Beads of perspiration stood out on the captain's forehead. "Orders," he repeated feebly.

"Papa, you are being most uncivil," Delphie protested. "The captain is merely carrying out Colonel Charteris's wishes."

"Mars is wooing Venus." Miss Wigge declaimed archly. "Love must be served, my lord."

Lord Burgess blinked several times and managed a feeble, "Hey?"

"You did inform Colonel Charteris that he could call upon me," Delphie pointed out in a demure voice. "I am persuaded you know that the colonel is a romantic man."

The look on Lord Burgess's face awakened Patricia's sense of mischief. "Indeed, even a sensible man may wax romantic when his heart is involved."

Her uncle digested this for a moment. "Well, that's enough foolishness for one day," he said at last. "It's time to return to the house."

The ladies rose, and the young officer immediately fell in behind them. Lord Burgess regarded him with a dubious eye.

"Thought Charteris was a sensible man," he whispered loudly to Patricia. "It just goes to show you, hey? Never heard anything as silly as that poem. But," he added cheerfully, "I expect you can do any damned thing when you're as rich as Charteris."

Hurrying after the captain, he began solicitous inquiries about the colonel's health. Patricia slowed her steps until the others were out of earshot and then ducked down a side path that led toward the stables. A few moments with Seamus and Argos would be just the tonic she needed after the morning's madness.

She had not gone far when she heard a step behind her. Assuming that the captain had come after her, she spoke over her shoulder. "Pray tell my uncle that I will return to the house in a moment."

"Certainly if that's your wish."

Patricia felt herself going stiff and cold as though all the blood in her veins had turned to ice.

79

"Actually I doubt if your uncle would consider me a fit emissary," Lord Longe continued. "But in any event and in all things I am yours to command."

With a deliberation that she didn't feel, Patricia turned to face his lordship. He had doffed his curly beaver to her, and his hair glowed like dark silk in the March sunshine. He wore a caped gray riding coat of superb cut and held a whip in his gray-gloved fist. His lips curved in that maddening, self-assured smile.

"You resemble a rose this morning," Lord Longe commented.

But a prickly rose, he amended silently. It was the first time he had seen Patricia Surrey since she had cursed him so roundly, and nothing about her had softened. Her dark-lashed hazel eyes offered no quarter, and under her thick shawl, amber like her modish, high-waisted walking dress with Spanish sleeves, he could see her tensed for fight. Even her small hands, gloved in fawn kid to match her shoes, were clenched.

He waited for her to speak, but Patricia was determined not to utter a sound. Since he had made her lose her composure and disgrace herself by flinging Jack's oath at his head, she had resolved to have no further dealings with this man. Even though he came often—twice or three times a week—to see Freddy, she had managed to avoid him.

Managed, that is, until today. Ignoring the more than usual rapid beating of her heart, Patricia lifted her chin and squared her shoulders. She took a step forward and promptly tripped over a loose stone.

Lord Longe caught her by the arm and steadied

her. Solicitously he said, "It's unwise not to look where you are going."

She pulled free, but his handclasp seemed to linger on her arm like a bracelet of warmth. "Please to get out of my way," she snapped.

"I'm not in your way," Lord Longe pointed out reasonably. "If I don't mistake, you were walking toward the stables, which are over in that direction."

Gritting her teeth, Patricia began to walk again. He fell into step with her.

"You told me once that whenever things upset you, you need to get up on a horse. Has something happened to distress you?" She kept a determined silence, and after a moment he continued, "What were we talking about? Ah, yes, roses. Now, I don't pretend to know much about flowers, but roses are my favorites."

Patricia could not resist remarking, "Then you had best take care. Roses have thorns."

"That," he assured her, "is why they are my favorite flower."

She would not rise to his bait again, Patricia swore. She *would* not. But as she continued to walk, she was acutely aware that Lord Longe was watching her.

She could not know that he was thinking that he had never seen her look so lovely. The deep gold of her dress caught the exact color of her eyes, and her high color emphasized the beautiful line of her cheek. Yes, his lordship decided, Patricia Surrey was beautiful—and angry enough to call him out.

He stifled a sigh. "It's such a fine day that I mean to take Freddy for a drive in the curricle. Do you think that if I bundle the boy in blankets and shawls, I could persuade Lady Burgess to let him go with me?" When Patricia did not reply, he added philosophically, "Ah, well. If at first I don't succeed, I'll try again."

She glanced at him out of the corners of her eyes and saw that one dark eyebrow had slanted up. Looking directly at her, he drawled, "I intend to succeed."

Patricia turned so swiftly that her skirts whipped around her ankles. "You are an odious man," she breathed. "You are—"

"Contemptible?" He suggested helpfully. "Vile? Or perhaps you'd like to borrow a few phrases from Heeming, my groom. He might say I was a 'gauming, clouterly gobbin.'"

Imps of mischief danced in his eyes, and an answering laughter flooded into her throat. For a second Patricia forgot that she hated this man. For one moment she imagined herself back on the down. She was dressed in Freddy's hunt clothes, Argos was cropping grass nearby, and she had just met Lord Jonathan Longe. During one heartbeat's time Patricia actually felt happy again.

Then reality returned, and she was furious with herself. It was unthinkable that she should forget, even for a moment, that Lord Longshanks had nearly caused Jack's death or that because of him many young men of the Nineteenth Foot Guards had never returned from Talavera.

Her voice shook as she whispered, "No words are fit to describe you, my lord."

Patricia turned her back on the duke's son and practically ran for the stables. In silence he watched her go.

His strong face had turned grim, and his eyes

were hard. He was struggling to restrain himself from striding after this maddening woman. He wanted to pull her into his arms and kiss her breathlessly. That should wipe that disdainful look from her proud face.

Lord Longe actually took two steps forward before common sense reasserted itself. *Patience,* he urged himself as he turned around and began to make for Burgess Hall.

Patricia heard his retreating steps and felt heartfelt relief that his lordship had taken himself off. But though Lord Longe had gone, his curricle was very much in evidence at the stables. His groom had evidently been given orders not to keep the horses standing and was trotting the matched grays along the riding track.

Seamus, hands on hips, stood watching. "High steppers, the both of them," he approved.

Patricia agreed that she had never seen such fine animals. They were beautifully matched in color, and they had perfectly straight hocks and quarters well let down. "They are superb," she agreed.

"And himself can drive to an inch as I've seen this morning," Seamus continued. "He took that difficult corner at the gate house as sweetly as you please. He has light hands, has Lord Longe."

Patricia thought of his lordship's light heels—the ones that had earned him his nickname at Talavera. "I collect that you have been very busy with all this thinking," she said tartly.

"Oh, I have. Thinking's something that everybody should do once in a while."

Patricia felt herself rebuked. She wanted to put her head down on the old groom's shoulder and cry as she had done when she was a little girl and had been thrown from her first horse. As if he had read her thoughts, Seamus's tone gentled.

"Whist, now, Miss Patricia. Mr. Jack will be home soon, and then all will come to rights for you. Were you thinking of a ride, then, and Argos wanting to stretch his legs?"

"I do not know what I want," she admitted. Then, because she had to tell someone, she found herself adding, "He did not deny it, Seamus. He told me that he was—that he was Lord Longshanks and had called a retreat during the battle."

Seamus stuck out his underlip. "I've heard the song that the colonel's silly groom is singing at the White Dragon. A pity, I'm thinking. It's a fine-looking man is his lordship."

Patricia thought of Lord Longe's hand clasping her arm a few moments ago. She remembered the support of his arm around her waist as they waltzed and the touch of his lips on her hand. She rubbed that hand absently, as if this could erase such treacherous memories.

Watching her, Seamus was worried. The young mistress hadn't looked so troubled since Mr. Jack had come back wounded.

His age and his arthritic bones had conspired to keep Seamus in Somerset during the war, when he would have much rather been with Mr. Jack. Even so, he knew a thing or two about fighting. He cleared his throat to say, "War's different than what you picture it, Miss Patricia. It's not parades and pretty uniforms at all, at all. Sometimes awful things happen during a battle, and people do things they don't mean to. Holy saints—Mr. Jack'd be the first to tell you that."

"I wish he were back, Seamus. Oh, I wish he were back."

Patricia brushed the back of her hand across her suddenly wet eyes. She placed a hand against the old man's arm for a moment before beginning to walk back to the house. Her eyes were still blurred with tears and she was so deep in her thoughts that she did not hear or see Freddy until he had rushed around a corner of the garden path and collided with her.

"Good heavens," Patricia exclaimed as they disentangled themselves. "Where are you going in such a hurry?"

Freddy was in his shirtsleeves and shivering with cold and temper. "Don't you st-start with me, Pat," he cried. "It's m-more than a fellow can stand. Lord Longe came all this way in his c-curricle to fetch me, but that s-sneak Mimsby peached on me again—said I'd c-coughed this morning—and Mama s-says it's too cold for me to ride out. I tell you, I had to get out of there quickly, or I'd have blown up."

He would have gone on except that he suddenly recalled their supposed feud. "I beg your pardon," he said stiffly.

Patricia put her hands on her hips and cried, "You are a great wigeon, Freddy. Why do you act as if I am your enemy?"

"You're the wigeon," he retorted scornfully. "How c-can you believe that a man l-like Lord Longe could be the coward of T-Talavera?"

"Captain Farell said—"

"That gull-catcher! He's just repeating what Charteris t-tells him. Pat, you're not such a want-wit that you'd t-take the colonel's word?"

Patricia conjured up an image of the colonel. The

puffed-up, pompous figure did little to recommend itself. "But Lord Longe admitted that he was Lord Longshanks," she murmured.

Even this did not shake Freddy's conviction. "If any f-female'd accused me of being c-cow-hearted, I'd have been as mad as fire. I'd have told her to believe what she liked. Men have their p-pride, Pat."

As Freddy spoke, footsteps sounded nearby. Patricia half expected Lord Longe to appear around a cluster of topiary bushes, but it was only Captain Farell making for the stables. He had tucked his lute under his arm and his cloak billowed about him, exposing his picturesque costume.

"You b-believe *him*, do you?" Freddy exclaimed sarcastically. "Delphie'll be making him j-jump through hoops next."

Frowning her cousin into silence, Patricia inquired, "Are you leaving so soon, Captain?"

The captain sent a fulminating look over his shoulder. "I have no choice. That fellow arrived awhile back—refuse to stay in the same house with him, don't you know."

Freddy bristled. "Are you s-speaking of Lord Longe?"

The young officer looked down his handsome nose and said scornfully, "Insufferable fellow—doesn't know when he's not wanted."

"For your information, Lord Longe has come to visit *m-me*." Freddy drew himself to his full five feet and six inches. "I consider his lordship m-my friend."

The captain looked astonished, then affected a condescending tone. "You're young, Harmon—don't know the world—fellow's besmirched. Not good to be tarred by the same brush, eh? Word to the wise will do."

"No, it won't," Freddy knuckled his hands into fists. "If you s-say one more thing about Lord Longe, I'll c-call you out!"

"Freddy!" Patricia exclaimed.

"I m-mean it. I won't have anyone t-treat Lord Longe rudely in my presence."

Freddy stepped forward and poked a finger into the young officer's shirt front. "Next t-time you malign Lord Longe, I'm going to send you my cartel."

Disdainfully the captain attempted to walk around Freddy, who promptly blocked his way. "Take a damper, young bantam," he snapped.

Freddy shook a fist under the captain's handsome nose. "If you d-don't meet me, I'll t-tell everyone you're c-cow-hearted."

The captain flushed red. "Now, look here," he was beginning, when Patricia intervened.

"Captain, you must not regard what my cousin says. He is tongue-valiant, as both his sister and I know well."

She watched as the implications of her speech trickled slowly through the captain's brain. Patricia could see indignation being replaced first by uncertainty and then by alarm.

The captain had realized how disastrous it would be to come to cuffs with the brother of his adored Delphinium. With a visible effort he retrenched and regrouped.

"No need to take that tone, Harmon," he said stiffly. "Only considering your best interests, don't you know."

"Well, you d-don't have to. Too many d-dashed people are watching out for my best interests. I'm s-sick of the lot of them." Freddy's eyes glinted with a martial light as he added, "Just leave Lord Longe alone."

Holding himself as straight as a lance, he marched back toward the house. When Patricia followed, he glanced at her out of the corners of his eyes. "If you're g-going to blow me up, Pat," he growled, "I ain't g-going to listen."

"Nothing of the kind. I think it courageous of you to take up the cudgels for someone you feel is your friend." Patricia hesitated before adding, "But just because Lord Longe is pleasant to you and—and offers to take you riding in his curricle, it does not prove him worthy of your regard. Remember what he is."

Freddy snorted. "You f-females don't know everything."

Chapter Six

"**V**ery witty, upon my word," Lord Burgess declared. "You know how to tell a story, Charteris. Hey, m'dear?"

"If you say so, sir," Delphie muttered.

Lady Burgess bent a keen look upon her bored daughter. As the mad March weather had settled, Colonel Charteris had finally rid himself of his cold. He now visited Burgess Hall as often as his secretary had once done. Unfortunately Delphinium did not seem particularly pleased. Though prettier than ever today in a spring-green dress of striped muslin, she looked undeniably sullen.

Lady Burgess recalled what her husband had said just last night. "Mark my word, Maria," his lordship had warned, "the chit will be sorry for her Friday face. Charteris is a big catch on the marriage market. Hey? As soon as the Season starts, all the London mamas will be throwing their caps at him."

Delphinium was being a peagoose to treat the colonel in so cavalier a fashion. Of course, Lady Burgess reasoned, the girl was too young to entertain any *serious* thoughts of marriage. But though Delphinium was pretty enough to *take* after her come out, a suitor such as Colonel Charteris could only add to her consequence.

In fact, any eligible gentleman with wealth, property, connections to Teglare, *and* the ear of the Viscount Wellington could not be taken lightly. Lady Burgess smiled ingratiatingly upon the colonel, who had launched into yet another long-winded anecdote, then frowned at her daughter. The foolish girl wasn't even troubling to conceal her yawns.

If only she would emulate dear Patricia. Her ladyship glanced fondly at her niece without guessing that Patricia was fast asleep with her eyes open.

It was a skill Jack had cultivated at Harrow and which he had taught his sister. It had come in useful these past days. Forced, along with her cousins, to endure visits from the colonel, Patricia had spent most of her time dreaming. As Colonel Charteris prosed on and on now, she fancied herself riding the downs with Jack.

The downs were green and beautiful, and it was so good to hear Jack's laughter. She turned to look at her brother, and was startled to see that her companion was Lord Longe.

Patricia blinked back to reality and heard Delphie say, "I collect, Papa, that you told me that you and the colonel were going to a wild beast show at Pelham-on-Wye."

What had happened, Patricia wondered, to make

her aunt look so displeased? She glanced at Freddy, who was standing moodily in a corner, and at Delphie's mutinous face. "I am persuaded that you will be late. You should leave at once," Delphie was continuing.

"So we should, Miss Harmon," the colonel boomed. "A wild beast show in that paltry village will no doubt be provincial entertainment, but, 'That is the very thing to wile away a dull afternoon in the country,' I told myself."

Somewhat wistfully Lord Burgess said, "After the exciting life you've led, Charteris, Sussex must seem tame. Hey? You must long for London."

"Certainly London is much more entertaining than the country, but now my heart would remain in Sussex." The colonel cast a speaking look at Delphie. "I say this even though I mislike having Longe as a neighbor."

Lord Burgess looked uneasily at the door. There was always the possibility that *that fellow* might walk through the door.

He'd done everything he could to discourage those visits. Though the baronet did not dare to actually *forbid* a duke's son entry to his house, he had become increasingly rude. And yet the man continued to plague Burgess Hall with his presence.

Perhap he was on his way here at this very moment. Lord Burgess cleared his throat and said, "Perhaps we'd better be on our way. Is Farell coming with us?"

Patricia noticed that Delphie, who had been staring boredly at the ceiling, suddenly began to pay attention.

"Farell has too much work to do. Letters need to be answered—important letters," the colonel added significantly, "from the Viscount Wellington. 'Farell,' I said, 'make sure these are written by this evening and ready for my signature.' Unlike a man whose name would insult present company, I do not shirk my duty."

He bowed to the ladies and strode off in Lord Burgess's wake. As Lady Burgess signaled Freddy to follow, Delphie whispered, "If we remain here, Mama will eat me for behaving rudely to that boring man. Help me escape, Patricia."

This Patricia did by begging her cousin to write something in a letter to Jack. The young ladies left the drawing room hurriedly and were silent until they had reached Delphie's chamber. Here Delphie plopped down on her bed and made a face at the door.

"I do so wish the colonel would go to Jericho," she cried.

A burst of laughter rose from the courtyard. Patricia winced as she heard the colonel begin to whistle, " 'They shout it high, they shout it low, they shout it far and near-o—' "

"Indeed, he is an abominable creature," she agreed.

"I loathe Colonel Charteris as much as you despise Lord Longe, Patricia."

" '—The coward of Talaver-o,' " the colonel whistled.

"It is a great pity they do not shoot each other," Patricia exclaimed.

There seemed to be no hope of this happening. If that song were being sung about her, Patricia thought, she would not have remained quiet for an instant. She would have handed the colonel her cartel long ago—or she would have thrashed him.

The fact that Lord Longe had done nothing was all the more proof that the stories about him were true.

"And yet," she mused, "there appear to be many people who do not believe the colonel. Can it be only because of his father that Lord Longe continues to be received everywhere?"

Delphie shrugged. "I cannot but wonder why he keeps coming here. Yesterday when he came to take Freddy out for a ride in his curricle, Papa was unutterably rude to him."

What Lord Burgess had said was, "Some people don't know when they're not wanted. Hey? A pity such fellows can't be swatted away like black flies."

Patricia narrowed her eyes. "If someone spoke to me like that, I—I should—Delphie, *what* are you doing?"

Her cousin had seated herself at her mirror and was engaged in swabbing a yellowish liquid all over her face.

"It is Mama's distillation of pineapples for wrinkles," she explained. "Pray do not go into whoops, Patricia. Look here—I have found a wrinkle."

"Delphie, you goose. I do not see anything."

"It is there nonetheless. Grief at being separated from my Arthur is having its affect." Delphie looked suddenly mournful. "We have not spoken together in a week. The last time we saw each other was in our drawing room, and the colonel kept shouting all the time."

Delphie set down the distillation of pineapples with a thump. "I am sick of the colonel and everyone else," she announced. "Patricia, let us go riding."

"But I thought you disliked horses!"

"A wrinkle on one's face calls for drastic measures." Delphie rose decisively from her mirror. "Also, it is cloudy today and I have heard that fog is good for the complexion. Do you not wish to ride, Patricia?"

Patricia went to the French windows, opened them, and stepped out onto Delphie's little balcony. Far away stretched the downs, and Patricia recalled her dream of riding with Jack. And then the dream had changed—

She let her breath out in an exasperated little sigh, and Delphie came out to slip an arm around her waist. "There, you see? You, too, are sick of being cooped up in the house." Sympathetically she added, "I know how much you miss Jack."

But behind the now-familiar loneliness for her brother there was something more—something that nagged like a toothache. Patricia was suddenly impatient with herself. It was not like her to act in this missish fashion.

"You are right, Delphie," she exclaimed. "A brisk ride will put us both to rights. If you will ask Aunt Maria for permission, I will have Seamus saddle our horses."

Delphie was relieved to find her mother reading Lady Caroline Lamb's newest and most outrageous novel. Anxious to learn the latest scandal about the Ten Thousand, Lady Burgess did not deliver a lecture on deportment. "It may come on the mizzle" was all she said. "Remember that March weather is changeable."

Seamus, who was to accompany them, agreed with her ladyship's assessment. "Sure, and it looks like there's more rain in those clouds," he warned. "Best not ride far today, I'm thinking."

They started out immediately and once seated on Argos, Patricia felt better. The air was clean, cool, and moist; the road deserted under the gray sky. But as they turned a corner, a cloaked figure on horseback emerged from behind a tree.

"A highwayman!" Delphie shrieked.

Patricia laughed. "Do not be a wigeon. It is only Freddy."

Freddy was muffled up in a heavy riding coat, and his face was shadowed by a much too large riding hat. He looked pleased with himself. "I gave Mimsby the s-slip," he crowed. "Ain't he g-going to be hipped when he finds I'm gone? I hope Mama hands him a jaw-me-dead."

Delphie, who was looking none too pleased, demanded, "Then Mama does not know you are out and on a horse?"

"No, and you ain't g-going to tell her," her brother retorted. "If you d-do, I'll peach on you about that letter you g-got from Farell."

Delphie called her younger brother an odious beast and added, virtuously, that she had never received such a letter.

Freddy hooted. "You'll catch c-cold trying to gammon me. I saw you holding it mashed t-to your chest—like this—and I'll lay you a m-monkey it wasn't from the colonel." He grinned. "D-did the cabbage-head write you m-more ramshackle poetry?"

Hastily Patricia intervened. "Since you are here and warmly dressed, Freddy, you may as well come along. We are only riding a little way."

But when they crested the first down, they saw that they were not the only ones who had come out to ride. Captain Farell, attired in a sweeping black cloak, was patiently waiting for them on the downward slope. Somehow Patricia was not surprised to see him.

"You arranged to m-meet him," Freddy accused.

His sister tossed her head. "What of it? You are all here to chaperon me. And you will not tell Mama because if you do, *I* will inform her that you escaped Mimsby and that you were on a horse, and she will immediately banish you to your room with a footbath and a mustard plaster."

She paused to watch the effect of her words, but Freddy was staring at the captain. "Man's gone as mad as a hatter," he exclaimed. "L-look at him!"

Under his flowing black cape Captain Farell wore the hose and doublet that had been fashionable during the day of the Tudors. On his head was perched a flat cap such as had been worn in Shakespeare's time.

"Do not tell me that you have prevailed upon Captain Farell to dress up as Romeo!" Patricia laughed.

Delphie, all smiles now, nodded, and the captain doffed his hat and held it to his heart. As Delphie urged her mare forward, Seamus leaned toward his mistress.

"Glory be to God Almighty, I've seen it all," he breathed. "That gentleman is addled in the head, I'm thinking." He then added shrewdly, "Miss Patricia, your aunt's not going to like what's going on."

But Patricia was remembering the look in Delphie's eyes when she spoke of her Arthur. "What harm can there possibly be to their meeting? Captain Farell is received at Burgess Hall, after all, and all of us are here to play chaperon."

Besides, even in his ridiculous attire the captain was far more pleasant than his superior officer. Patricia felt no remorse as she trotted Argos up to the captain and Delphie, who cried, "Patricia, is it not wonderful that Captain Farell chose to ride today? Do let us go on toward the river. It is so very beautiful there."

"Yoicks!" Freddy shouted.

Joyously pounding his heels into his horse's side, he cantered away. Patricia followed. It was, she reflected, wonderful to be on a horse. With so much rain last month, there had been little time to ride. No wonder she had felt so full of megrims and humors.

She was so lost in the pleasure of riding that it was some time before she looked about her. Then she realized that they had passed the fork in the road and were riding east toward the Leads River. Some distance ahead of them lay Riverway.

The sight of Lord Longe's estate evoked unpleasant memories. But when Patricia suggested turning back, Delphie protested this. "It is such a beautiful day for riding. Do you not think so, Arth— I mean, Captain Farell?"

"Permit me to say—any day spent in your company—heavenly."

As the captain turned his besotted eyes on Delphie, Patricia felt a drop of moisture on her cheek. She glanced upward and realized that the hitherto overcast skies had turned almost black.

She exclaimed, "It is going to rain. Oh, why did we come so far? We must turn back at once." Raising her voice she called, "Freddy, we must go!"

But Freddy, who was enjoying his hour of freedom, did not or would not heed her. "I'll go after him, Miss Patricia," Seamus offered.

Patricia shook her head. "He might argue with you, and there is no time to lose. Please turn back with the captain and Miss Harmon, Seamus, and I will bring Freddy with me."

At her command Argos bounded forward. "Freddy," Patricia shouted. "It is time to turn back."

Still her cousin did not hear. Patricia urged her gelding to greater speed. Suddenly the heavens blazed with light, and a shaft of lightning stabbed down. It was immediately followed by a crack of thunder.

Startled, Argos reared up on his haunches. As Patricia brought him under control, she saw that Freddy was also struggling to master his bucking horse.

Another flash of lightning, a second roar of thunder—and then the rain began. In the near-blinding downpour, Patricia realized that her cousin was losing his battle to control his horse. "Hold fast, Freddy," she cried. "Oh, heavens!"

For Freddy's frightened horse had bolted. Neighing its fear, it pounded up a sharp incline beyond which lay the river.

Patricia tucked down her head and applied the spurs. Argos made a gallant effort, but even this was not enough. Patricia knew she would not be in time to reach Freddy before his horse reached the riverbank.

And the boy could not hold on. He was bobbing and weaving in the saddle. He would be thrown into the river, and she could not prevent it—

Someone, riding like the wind, passed her by, and

a storm-shadowed form on a powerful horse thundered toward Freddy. He had reached the youth, grasped his bridle, and turned his horse by the time Patricia came galloping up.

"Thank heavens that you came," she cried.

"It was merest chance I was near," a familiar voice replied.

Patricia stared at Lord Longe and blurted, "What are *you* doing here?"

"It's my land," he explained mildly.

He turned to the trembling Freddy and remarked cheerfully, "That was some ride, young 'un—neck-or-nothing all the way."

A watery chuckle was wrung from Freddy, but his smile died almost at once. "My horse did a b-bolt," he croaked. "If it wasn't for you, sir, I'd have been finished."

Lord Longe denied this, but Patricia knew her cousin spoke truly. Freddy's mad ride had taken him almost to the lip of the riverbank. It was high ground here, and there were jagged rocks below. If Freddy had been thrown onto those rocks—

She turned frightened eyes to Lord Longe, who, still holding Freddy's bridle, was drawing the horse away from the riverbank. "That crack of lightning caught even Sultan by surprise," he said calmly. "No wonder your horse bolted, Harmon. Are you and Miss Surrey riding alone today?"

Distractedly Patricia recalled the others. "Delphie and Captain Farell are with us as is Seamus," she said. "They must be on the road home by now. I said that I would overtake Freddy and join them."

But she had not been able to catch up to her cousin, would never have reached him before he was

99

thrown. Patricia thought of those waiting rocks and felt physically ill.

"It's all right." Patricia was so distressed that she did not realize Lord Longe had taken her hand. "There's nothing to fear," he continued. "It's only a storm."

He could feel her small hand tremble in his. With difficulty Lord Longe restrained himself from putting a protective arm about Patricia's shoulders.

"Farell will see to Miss Harmon," he went on, "so they'll be all right. If you'll ride on the other side of your cousin, Miss Surrey, I'll guide you to Riverway Place."

At mention of Lord Longe's home Patricia realized where her hand still lay. Hastily withdrawing it from his lordship's clasp, she protested, "No, that will not do. Aunt Maria will be worried to death if the others return without us. We must return to Burgess Hall."

"In that case, I'll ride with you." When she protested this, he added, "You're not as familiar with the way as I am and might become lost in the downpour. I know the downs like the back of my hand."

Patricia did not argue further, and Lord Longe blessed the chance that had made him ride out on this gloomy day. He had spent the morning at the Yanceys' country estate, but though Percival had urged him to remain for luncheon, he had felt too restless to sit through the small talk of a meal. If he had stayed or if he had been a few moments later—

"My cousin would have been gravely hurt had you not come when you did." Patricia spoke in a low tone so Freddy could not hear her as she added, "You put yourself in danger to save him."

"You make too much of it. Anyway, you would have reached him in time." She shook her head in denial, but he added warmly, "I've seldom seen such a bruising ride. And this time there was no hedge to stop you."

She gave a little gulp that could have been a chuckle. "Once again you came to the rescue, it seems."

In spite of the cold rain and her recent terror, Patricia realized that she was feeling absurdedly lighthearted. It was, she reasoned, because Freddy was safe. But any illusion of safety disappeared as the storm worsened. The wind dashed sheets of wind into their faces and made it almost impossible to see, and the lightening was blinding. The horses stumbled on treacherous and slippery ground and whinnied their fear. Freddy's mount might have bolted again if Lord Longe had not held his bridle and talked soothingly to the beast.

How could the man remain so calm? Patricia wondered, as she listened to his lordship joking with Freddy. She herself felt all on the jump each time a lightning bolt seared the darkness. She had never seen such a storm much less been in one, and if Lord Longe hadn't offered to escort them, she was sure that they would have lost their way and wandered hopelessly around the downs.

It was what had befallen the others. Some ten minutes later, when they came upon the little group, they were riding the wrong way. Delphie was sobbing hysterically, and her dripping cavalier, who was trying unsuccessfully to calm her, was not paying attention to Seamus's entreaties and exhortations.

"Miss Patricia—Holy saints, I was after fearing you were swallowed up in the storm." Seamus drew closer to add out of the corner of his mouth, "I have been trying to convince that captain that he's going the wrong way, but himself is as stubborn as a goat. It's glad I am to see you, Miss Patricia, and Mr. Harmon, and—"

He broke off, staring at Lord Longe. The captain now added peevishly, "Disoriented—can't see a thing in this rain—fool of a groom thinks he knows everything—"

Then he, too, became aware of Lord Longe. In the fraught silence that followed, Freddy explained what had happened. "Lord L-Longe s-saved me from a f-fall into the river," he added. "He s-saved my life."

"Not a bit of it. I will, however, save you from becoming even wetter," his lordship interrupted. "If all of you will follow me, I will guide you to Burgess Hall."

The captain drew himself upright in the saddle, but before he could reject this offer from such a man as Lord Longe, Delphie began to sob, "Arthur," she wailed, "please take me home."

Ignoring the captain, Lord Longe leaned closer to the frightened girl. "Heart up, Miss Harmon," he said bracingly, "You'll soon be seated by a roaring fire. Captain, take her bridle and ride behind me. Seamus, you and Mr. Harmon bring up the rear. Miss Surrey, if you will ride with me?"

Seamus's gray eyebrows twitched, but he gave his lordship a look of respect and did as he was told. Even the captain grudgingly followed orders, for he was in no position to question Lord Longe's leadership. Delphie was shaking and sobbing with fear and clinging to him, and what with soothing her and guiding her horse along, the captain had his hands full.

As for Freddy, he sounded almost jaunty as he recounted the story of his wild ride to Seamus. "I never s-saw such a rider," Patricia could hear him say. "D'you know that he c-came out of n-nowhere, like the wind? C-caught me just as I was going over the edge onto those rocks."

Patricia shuddered. "I have not thanked you yet for saving Freddy," she said in a low voice.

"Nonsense."

"It is not nonsense at all. It was bravely done." Noting the twitch of his lordship's fine lips, she repeated almost defiantly, "It was a brave thing to do."

"Fustian. Your cousin was in no danger from a paltry toss into the river. Percival Yancey and I have dived between those rocks for sport."

"Even so," Patricia said, "I must thank you."

"I don't want your thanks, Miss Surrey."

Startled, she turned to look into gray eyes that were no longer cool or self-assured. Patricia caught her breath at the naked emotion on Lord Longe's face.

"I want," he was saying, "only what you can give with your whole heart."

Patricia was battered by conflicting emotions that left her feeling weak. She did not know what to say, so she said nothing. Clutching her wet bridle tightly, she stared sightlessly in front of her.

They rode in silence through the scudding rain

103

until Lord Longe spoke abruptly. "You're home. The stables are over there."

Patricia did not dare to look at him. "I can see that," she said.

In an effort to gain control of herself, she spoke curtly, and hearing the supposed hostility in her voice, Lord Longe cursed himself for a fool. He had vowed not to go too quickly or press her in any way. He should not have spoken, and yet when she had looked at him like that—

It cost him an effort to speak as though nothing had happened. "I must be on my way. Pray give my compliments to your aunt."

Freddy now rode up. "Ain't you c-coming in?" When his lordship shook his head, he protested, "But I haven't thanked you p-properly, sir. Besides, to ride b-back in this storm is f-foolish."

Lord Longe grinned. "If you must know, I lack the courage to face Lady Burgess."

Freddy blanched. "Oh, Lord, you're right. Ain't she g-going to r-ring a peal over my head? And that toad, Mimsby, will m-make things horrid for me, too. P-Pat, you'll st-stand by me, won't you? You'll not d-desert a fellow."

Just then the captain and Delphie came riding up. As they passed, Farell hesitated. Then, turning back, he raised his hand in a salute. The grudging gesture of thanks brought a wry smile to Lord Longe's lips.

"Best you go in, Harmon," he urged. "Her ladyship awaits."

"Pat—?" Freddy pleaded.

In the few seconds it took to assure her cousin that she would stand by him, Patricia realized that Lord Longe had gone. The gray rain cloaked his broad-shouldered form immediately, and the sodden ground muffled Sultan's hoofbeats. But he left behind the question that had been burning in Patricia's mind for the past half hour.

How, Patricia wondered, was it possible that a man like Lord Jonathan Longe could have acted the coward at Talavera?

Chapter Seven

When she first set eyes on her dripping son, Lady Burgess almost expired from shock. Rallying, she initiated a whirlwind of activity and soon servants were running up and downstairs with hot water, warmed bricks, flannels, goosegrease, broths, possets, and medicine.

Even Dr. Norrow's assurances did not convince his terrified mother. Lady Burgess caused the affronted Mimsby to watch her offspring like a hawk, while she herself dosed him with infusions until Freddy protested that he would much rather have an inflammation of the lungs than drink any more medicine. Exasperated by such ingratitude, Lady Burgess swore that Freddy never again would mount a horse.

At this point Charms announced that Lord Longe had come to call.

Lord Burgess was in London overseeing the opening of the family's London townhouse and concluding arrangements for his daughter's come-out, so my lady received his lordship alone. It was a short interview which left her shaken.

That evening, for the first time in forty-eight hours, she allowed Freddy to join the family at dinner. "I must talk to you, my son," she began.

"What about?" asked her apprehensive child.

Lady Burgess's lips quivered. "I am *grieved* that you set out to ride without my consent. If it had not been for *dear* Lord Longe, you might have been drowned," she paused. "Perhaps he is right when he says that you should be taught to sit a horse like a gentleman."

Freddy's jaw dropped open. Delphie stared. Patricia exclaimed, "Are you funning, ma'am?"

Lady Burgess shot her niece a reproachful look. "Surely you cannot believe that I would joke about *such* a subject? Lord Longe suggested that inexperienced riders suffered mishaps. He may be right." Lady Burgess heaved a lugubrious sigh, "He suggested that to keep Freddy from danger in the future I should—I should allow him to take riding lessons. I believe that the time has come—"

She was interrupted by a wild whoop as Freddy rocketed out of his chair. He hugged his mother and started to caper about the dining room while Lady Burgess implored him to compose himself. "I cannot deny Lord Longe anything," she declared tragically. "Not only is he the son of the duke of Parton, but I owe him a debt that only a mother's sacrifice can pay."

Patricia recommended Seamus as a teacher. The old groom went to work with a will, and by the time Lord Burgess returned from London, Freddy was cantering very creditably about the estate.

The baronet was preoccupied and in no mood to admire his son's prowess. "About time he learned something useful," was all he said.

Exercise improved Freddy's appetite and ruddied his complexion, so that even his anxious mother could not find fault with him. Patricia noted that her cousin did not stutter so badly, that his walk had a new swagger to it, and that he actually dared to argue with the tyrannical Mimsby.

One fine late March morning, Miss Wigge suggested an excursion. "We could drive into the village of Pelham-on-Wye," she suggested. "That is not far, and the old Norman church is most picturesque."

Delphie protested that she had seen this hideous old ruin at least fifty times, but her governess was undaunted.

"I collect, my love, that you have the megrims from staying indoors too long. It is a fine day, and dear Miss Surrey can drive us in the phaeton. Perhaps Mr. Harmon may be prevailed upon to act as our escort. After all," Miss Wigge added archly, "it is spring, it is spring, hey nonny-nonny-no!"

Patricia was agreeable. Freddy, eager to show off his horsemanship, was easily persuaded. Delphie made it plain that it was all one to her if they went to Pelham-on-Wye or to China. Patricia noted, however, that her cousin put on her new periwinkle-blue pelisse and perched a modish bonnet, trimmed with silk violets, on her golden curls.

"You look like a fairy princess, my love," Miss Wigge effused. "And you, Miss Surrey—moss-green is indeed your color. How well that bonnet becomes you, to be sure, with that saucy curling feather!" She tittered and clasped her hands to her bosom. "I collect that Mr. Harmon is escorting the graces today."

Contriving to fit three ladies in a phaeton caused a tight squeeze, but it was accomplished, and soon they were bowling along the road across the downs. As they progressed under an almost-cloudless sky, Freddy trotted his gelding around to Patricia's side.

"Wanted to ask you, Pat," he said, "if you noticed how Tyburn-faced the pater's been lately."

"He has certainly seemed preoccupied," Patricia agreed.

"While he was in London, he probably visited all the gambling hells. I'll lay you a m-monkey that he's plucked cleaner than a fowl ready for the s-stew pot," Freddy said. "I know the signs. Delphie does, too."

Patricia glanced at Delphie, who was gazing abstractedly across the downs and paying little attention to Miss Wigge's endless quotations about nature.

"That would explain why Uncle Hector avoids talk of London," Patricia mused. "Whenever Aunt brings up the subject of the Season or makes further plans for Delphie's come-out, he changes the subject."

She was interrupted by a deep sigh from Delphie. "Do you have the headache?" Patricia asked sympathetically.

"He has not been to visit since that day we were lost in the storm," Delphie murmured. "He was so strong, so resourceful, so *courageous*."

"Got the wrong man, ain't you?" her brother scoffed. "If it wasn't for Lord Longe, you'd probably s-still be lost."

"Patricia, can it be that he has lost interest in me?"

Delphie sounded so genuinely unhappy that Patricia felt a stab of sympathy. "I am sure that is not the case," she said gently.

Miss Wigge coughed delicately and quoted, " 'Stay me with flagons, comfort me with apples, for I am sick of love.' "

"I should think Farell is sick of it," Freddy interposed. "S-stands to reason, don't it? Poor bleater had to d-dress up like Prince Charming and write drivel—no wonder he's done a bolt."

Delphie wailed. Freddy laughed. The horses pricked up their ears and snorted. Patricia frowned at one cousin, soothed the other, and attended to her driving. But her busy hands did not keep her mind from drifting—not toward Delphie's captain but to Lord Longe.

Since his interview with her aunt, his lordship had not come to Burgess Hall. Patricia told herself she was grateful that this was the case, for Freddy's rescue had changed nothing. Lord Longe was still someone she despised. Determinedly Patricia suppressed the memory of ardent gray eyes and a deep voice that had begun to disturb her dreams.

"Oh, mercy!" Delphie shrieked.

Instinctively Patricia reined in the horses. Though still some distance from the village with its thatched-roof cottages and neat gardens, they had reached Pelham-on-Wye's public house. This was a large, cheerful establishment with a steady clientele of farmers, sheep men, and merchants. Certainly there was nothing about it to startle anyone.

Freddy demanded, "What'd you squeal for, you

gudgeon? It's only the White Dragon, and—oh, Lord, now we're in the s-soup."

Patricia had also recognized Colonel Charteris's groom. The man was attending to his master's coal-black gelding and Captain Farell's roan horse.

"Quick," Freddy urged. "We have to do a bolt before he s-sees us."

Fortune favored them. The colonel's groom had been distracted by a shabby old fellow who had stopped to ask a question. But as Patricia called softly to the horses, Delphie clutched her arm.

"Do not move on," she pleaded. "I must see *him*."

As she spoke, the inn door was flung open. Freddy groaned as the colonel came striding out, goggled at the phaeton, and then made straight for it.

"Servant, ladies," he boomed. "What brings the charming fair to this godforsaken village?"

Patricia wanted nothing more than to drive on, but to do so would be unforgivably rude. She sat silently as Delphie asked the question that was paramount on her mind.

"Farell? Oh, he's somewhere about. Good fellow, Farell, though not very efficient. He's been given to daydreaming lately, and I must tell you that I have regretted the loss of Philip Oranger, who was with me at Talavera. Miss Harmon, did I ever tell you about the time when the Viscount Wellington envied me my aide? 'Charteris,' the Viscount said, 'I envy you, Char—' "

The colonel stopped in midword. His self-satisfied smile disappeared. Patricia, following the direction of his gaze, saw that Lord Longe's curricle was fast approaching. Beside Lord Longe sat a round-faced gentleman in a stylish riding coat with many shoulder capes.

"What's *he* doing here?" Colonel Charteris growled.

Ignoring the colonel, Lord Longe drove his grays next to Patricia's phaeton and doffed his curly beaver.

"Your servant, ladies. Miss Harmon, I believe that you know Mr. Percival Yancey. Miss Surrey, may I present my friend?"

"Ladies, you need not speak to this man," the colonel interrupted.

Mr. Yancey raised a quizzing glass to his eye and said "Bedad!" in an astonished voice.

"Desist," continued the colonel in a voice loud enough to be heard by a cluster of farmers on the tavern steps. "These ladies are under my protection."

Very deliberately Lord Longe turned his head. "Was that to my address?" he wondered.

In spite of his even tone, Lord Longe was on the brink of losing his temper. Disguising the fact that his fingers itched to close around Charteris's thick throat, he drawled, "How pleasant it must be to have the protection of so honorable a man."

The words and the tone in which they were uttered were like a slap in the face. As the colonel turned a rich burgundy color, Freddy heaped coals on the fire. "My s-sister don't need your protection, Colonel," he said. "She's with *m-me*."

Keenly aware that several other patrons of the public house had appeared on the steps, Patricia interposed. "We are on our way to visit the Norman church and cannot stop any longer," she said firmly. "Good day, gentlemen."

She urged the horses forward, but before she could drive more than a few yards, there was an explosive sound behind them. "Get away from me, you clod!" the colonel shouted.

Patricia whipped her head around and saw that the colonel was not addressing Lord Longe. The object of his rage was the old man who had been speaking earlier to his groom.

The old fellow had whipped off his cap, and his tattered gray hair danced in the March breezes. "You ain't got no call to talk to me that way, guv'nor," he was protesting. "Just harsking for work, I am. Halways worked for me shilling, I 'ave, even though I got this 'ere bum leg in the war."

The colonel harrumphed. "Your kind never works. All you can do is whine to your betters. Be off before I take my crop to you."

As he turned his back, the old fellow caught at the colonel's sleeve. "Sir, I come all this way to harsk you—"

His only answer was a cut from the colonel's riding crop. "Shame!" Patricia cried.

She drew rein and would have climbed down from the phaeton, but Miss Wigge caught her arm. "Miss Surrey," she quavered, "pray let us drive on. This is no place for ladies."

The colonel's whip hand rose again. Shaking off Miss Wigge's hand, Patricia jumped to the ground and started back toward the White Dragon. Behind her, she heard Freddy call out a warning, but she did not heed him.

"Stop beating that man," she ordered the colonel.

Lord Longe had been on the point of driving away when he heard Patricia cry out. As he checked his grays, he heard the colonel snarl, "This will teach you to manhandle your betters."

This time the colonel's whip descended with such

113

force that the old man fell to his knees. Charteris raised his arm for a third blow, but it never fell.

"Enough," Lord Longe said.

He tore the riding crop from the colonel's grasp and flung it onto the ground.

Just then, Patricia came running up. Casting a look of contempt at the colonel, she bent to help the old man. As she did so, she heard Lord Longe say, "Beating an old man is hardly sport."

His hard gray eyes met Charteris's protuberant green ones squarely. "Get out of my way," the colonel blustered. "Who are you to interfere with me?"

"Bedad, best you take a damper, old boy." Mr. Yancey had alighted from the curricle and was perambulating languidly forward. "Look at all the cits staring," he continued. "Bad *ton* to brawl in front of an inn, Chateris. Very bad."

Freddy had now ridden up. He dismounted and ranged himself beside Lord Longe.

Finding so many unfriendly eyes fixed on him, the colonel clamped shut his mouth, turned on his heel, and roared for his horse. "Farell, where the hell are you?" he bellowed.

The captain came running out of the White Dragon. He saw Delphie sitting in the phaeton some distance away and stopped as though transfixed. A long, eloquent look passed between them before the colonel commanded his secretary to mount up. "Why are you never there when you're needed?" he shouted.

As the colonel vented his frustration on his secretary, Lord Longe addressed the man Charteris had been beating. "Are you hurt?" he asked.

The old fellow shook his head. "I was only harsking for a job. A bit down on me 'ealth and me luck 'asn't been good since the Peninsula."

"An old soldier?"

"Amos Owens is me name. Hartillery, I was, and in the thick o' it, too."

Patricia said, "You have been treated shamefully, Mr. Owens. I have no money with me, but if you come to Burgess Hall, I will make sure you have a good meal and some warm clothes."

"But that will not give you work," Lord Longe interposed. "There's need for an under gardener at Riverway. Is that to your liking?"

Owens beamed. "Thank yer, guv'nor. That suits me to the ground in a manner o' speaking. I'll get me things an' follow yer." Then, as Colonel Charteris racketed by with the captain galloping at his heels, he shouted, "An' bugger the colonel."

"Here, I say, ladies's present," Mr. Yancey protested, but Patricia would have none of it.

"I agree with Mr. Owens entirely—Colonel Charteris is a bully." She turned to Lord Longe adding, "I am very glad you were here, my lord, but I wish you had drawn that counter-coxcomb's claret."

Mr. Yancey looked astonished at such frank speech from a lady. Freddy grinned appreciatively. Lord Longe could think of nothing to say, for his only coherent thought was that Patricia Surrey was lovely.

Her bonnet had been pushed back as she ran, and the wind was busy ruffling her curls. Her eyes snapped with spirit, her cheeks were rosy. He could not look away from her, and under his gaze, a rueful smile curved her lips.

"I am much too tongue-valiant," she sighed.

Lord Longe forgot that he was standing in front

of an inn and that at least three dozen people were listening to every word he said. "You are perfect," he assured her.

His voice was like a caress. The sound of it affected Patricia's knees, which seemed suddenly to go weak. It was as though she could not tear her eyes away from Lord Longe.

They continued to gaze at each other until Mr. Yancey's diffident cough broke the spell. "No wish to interrupt, Jonathan, but is this fellow, Owens, to ride pillion behind your groom?"

Patricia was jolted back to reality. Suddenly aware of the number of interested onlookers who had gathered around them, she also realized that Freddy was plucking at her arm.

"B-best we get on, Pat," he urged, "Wiggy is threatening to have s-spasms, and Delphie don't look so pleased neither."

"And we must be on our way. Come, Percival." Lord Longe's smile did not quite hide his regret, as his eyes sought Patricia's again. Almost he held out his hand to take hers but dropped it to his side again. "I wish you a pleasant afternoon, ma'am," he said.

It wasn't till they had gone their separate ways that Patricia realized that she had smiled back at Lord Longshanks. For the space of a few moments they had been allies. Almost they had been friends. And when he had looked at her in that way—

Patricia didn't want to examine her feelings any further. She felt confused, almost frightened.

I must take care, she thought.

"I mislike the thought of your riding to hounds," Lady Burgess fretted. "Reflect, Patricia, that it is *not* a ladylike pursuit."

"But we are far from London society, and Uncle Hector does not object." When her aunt still looked unconvinced, Patricia added shamelessly, "And, after all, Freddy requested my presence. This is his first hunt—your birthday gift to him."

Lady Burgess raised her eyes to heaven. "Do not speak of Freddy's birthday," she exclaimed. "He tricked me into allowing him to ride to hounds. I am persuaded that you are in sympathy with him, Patricia."

Delphie came to her cousin's defense. "It was not Patricia's fault, Mama. It was all Freddy's idea to tease you until you said you would give him anything he wished for his birthday. And you did promise."

"I thought that he wanted to go to the Continent like his brother." Lady Burgess looked so distressed that Patricia hugged her.

"Do not be concerned, Aunt. Freddy will not come to harm."

Actually Patricia admired her cousin's daring. Not only had he been clever enough to get his mother to agree to let him join his father's next hunt, but he had stuck to his guns through days of recrimination, pleading, and even threats. Freddy was growing up.

Lady Burgess's attempts to enlist the aid of her spouse had failed. "Oh, let the boy hunt," Lord Burgess had growled. Then he had added incomprehensibly, "Might as well enjoy himself. Hey? All a man can do in this sorry world."

In her agitation Lady Burgess had not heeded this cryptic speech. "Well, perhaps he will not be hurt very badly," she had sighed.

Freddy could now be heard calling from the first floor. "Hurry, P-Pat, or we shall be late!"

Patricia adjusted the sleeves of her blue velvet riding dress, decorated à la hussar with frogs and epaulets. She set her matching shako, crowned with a curly ostrich feather, on her brown curls and picked up her leather gloves.

"D-don't you look fine," Freddy exclaimed as she came down the stairs.

So did her cousin, Patricia thought. His new-found muscle and weight did justice to his hunt clothes. As Lord Longe had predicted, they had not come to harm.

Sternly repressing memories of that meeting, Patricia spoke cheerfully. "Indeed, you are in the tweak of fashion, Freddy. The fox will expire from admiration."

Chatting companionably, they went outside to the stables where Lord Burgess, resplendent in scarlet coat, white stock, and black velvet cap, was stamping officiously about and bullying his underlings.

He gave his son a look of grudging approval and growled, "Well, you *look* the part. But I warn you that if you take a tumble, we're not waiting for you. Hey? I'm after that plaguey dog fox, and I ain't going to be put off today of all days."

Patricia wondered at the expression on her uncle's chubby features. He didn't look as though he was looking forward to a hunt. In fact, he looked positively hagridden.

"Where the devil's Charteris?" Lord Burgess continued irritably. "Man said he'd be here by ten. It's past the hour now."

Mumbling under his breath, he trotted off to give orders to his master of kennels who also acted as his huntsman. Freddy cocked a knowing eye after his father.

"The pater must really be beside the b-bridge this time," he observed. "I never saw him so hipped before." He paused to groan as a solitary rider came cantering into view. "Oh, worse luck, here comes Charteris. I'd been hoping he wouldn't s-show."

Patricia also wished that the boorish colonel were not joining Freddy's first hunt. "It cannot be helped, and—but that is not Colonel Charteris!"

Freddy's face lit up. "I didn't know Lord Longe was joining the hunt."

"He's not," Lord Burgess growled. "I'll not have that fellow join *my* hunt."

"But," Freddy pointed out, "you did invite him, P-Pater."

"Hey?"

Flinching, Freddy still stood his ground. "When we first went t-to Riverway, you s-said that he must hunt with you."

Lord Burgess could only glower as the duke's son approached, but if Lord Longe felt the waves of hostility flowing toward him, he ignored them. His greetings were courtly, his bearing without fault. Patricia couldn't help but admire the powerful figure his lordship cut in his handsomely tailored black coat and cream-colored breeches.

It couldn't be that she was glad to see him. That would be too ridiculous to think on. Yet Patricia's heartbeat quickened as Lord Longe dismounted and walked over to her.

"Finally Miss Surrey," he said. "I'll be allowed to watch your prowess on the field."

Patricia couldn't help smiling, and seeing that smile, Lord Longe's hopes soared. Though his unexpected appearance had surprised her, Patricia didn't appear angry that he had come.

"How is Mr. Owens?" she was asking.

"Settling down. He's London-bred, but he comes from farming stock and always had the hankering to work the ground. He says he's happier pruning roses than he was firing cannon."

The friendly light in Patricia's eyes died. Without another word, she turned her back and walked away. Lord Longe checked an impulse to stop her from going, for he knew it to be useless.

One mention of the war, and the wall built by Charteris's lies rose up between them, and he had no idea of how to go about smashing that wall. Lord Longe had come to his neighbor's hunt because he'd learned that Charteris was also riding to hounds. A few days ago in the village, the colonel had lost his temper and made a fool of himself. Lord Longe hoped that if the man were pressed hard enough, he might do something to unmask his lies.

A halloo now resounded over the downs, and the colonel, followed by Captain Farell, came trotting toward them. Lord Longe noted with distaste that even at this distance Colonel Charteris seemed to sit his horse unsteadily. The man was either an incompetent rider or he was drunk.

The colonel's voice was slurred as he greeted the master of the hunt. He then goggled at Patricia. "Sher—servant, Miss Surrey. I wasn't aware you were joining us. Pleash—pleasure, I'm sure."

Lord Longe wanted to thrash Charteris for his condescending tone and the way he was leering at

Patricia. As he stepped forward, the smile froze on the colonel's lips.

"What's *he* doing here, Burgess?" he demanded.

The baronet wished his unwelcome guest in Jericho. He drew the colonel aside and explained in his carrying whisper. "I can't help it. Hey? I invited the fellow to hunt with me before I knew what he was. Can't renege now."

Patricia listened in disgust. She would have gladly left the hunt, but she did not want to spoil things for Freddy. She resolved that she would do her best to ignore the colonel, her uncle, and above all Lord Longe.

She stayed close to her cousin as the small party mounted up and moved away to the draw, which was a covert on the slope of the nearest down. As the hounds began to draw the thick grass, Patricia noticed that Freddy was looking a little pale.

"Battle nerves," he confessed with a shaky grin. "M'first hunt, you know. Lord Longe said I might feel that way, though." When she did not comment, he asked bluntly, "Are you s-sorry he's come?"

"I cannot be glad," she replied honestly.

Giving his cousin a disgusted look, Freddy wheeled his horse and rode to Lord Longe's side. Patricia saw the duke's son smile in welcome, and an ache that wasn't really an ache began in her chest.

"He is Lord Longshanks," she reminded herself. "I can never forget what he did."

The hounds' baying interrupted her, and a large dog fox broke nearby and began to run like the wind. "Gone away!" blew the huntsman's horn, and Lord Burgess yelped, "There's that bugger!"

The hunt began in earnest. Patricia, who usually

rejoiced in the feel of the wind in her face and the pace of Argos beneath her, couldn't seem to lose herself in the hunt. Not so Lord Burgess.

"Got him this time," he yodeled. "I've been chasing that beast for years. Hey? Hey? Today I'll have his tail!"

With the hounds in hot pursuit, the fox raced along the downward slope. Lord Burgess's exultant cries rose toward heaven. Then, suddenly, the fox vanished.

One moment there had been a streak of tawny gold against the emerald green grass—then there was nothing. The colonel slowed his black gelding and looked around, bewildered. "Did the fox go to earth?"

"No he ain't," the baronet snapped. "Oh, bloody hell, the little bastard's done it to me again!"

As the confused hounds began to sniff about, Patricia heard Lord Longe say, "If I was a betting man, I would put money on Reynard."

When last she'd seen him, he'd been riding with Freddy. She'd hoped that she could avoid him completely. Maintaining a frigid silence, Patricia turned Argos away.

He followed her. "What were we talking about before the hounds gave tongue?"

"I do not recollect that we had any conversation." But her blighting tone had little effect on his lordship.

"That's just as well. It's said that only true friends can be silent together. Although I have to admit 'friends' may not describe our relationship."

With difficulty she held her tongue. "And in any case," Lord Longe persisted, "friendship isn't what I hope for."

Patricia halted Argos and faced the duke's son directly. "I do not know what you are talking about, but I tell you to your head that I will never forgive you."

Calmly he replied, "But I don't expect you to forgive me."

"That is the first sensible thing I have ever heard you say!"

He hardly seemed to hear her. "How many hours do you think there are in one man's life?" he asked.

"How many—of course I do not know the answer to such an idiotish question."

"Well, for the sake of argument, let us assume that a man lives three score years and ten. That would make the sum of his days twenty-five thousand, five hundred days or five hundred and seventy-two thousand hours."

Lord Longe paused for a moment. "Can you tell me of one man—or woman, for that matter—who can live all those hours without having one moment of regret?"

She saw now where he was leading her. "That is no excuse," she exclaimed.

She had meant to say more, but something in his expression stopped her from uttering those cutting words. Suddenly Patricia felt confused and unhappy.

Lord Longe said quietly, "It is not intended to be an excuse, Miss Surrey."

At this moment Lord Burgess gave a yell.

"There! There he is, the mangy old bugger. Yee-up!"

Once more the hunt plunged on. Patricia urged Argos forward. She wanted to ride as fast as she could and get away from Lord Longe. She passed

Freddy, who was riding well, then Captain Farell, and finally Colonel Charteris, who was whipping his black gelding on. But though she did her best to outdistance him, Lord Longe kept easy pace with her.

They forded a brook, swept over dark-wooded hills, thundered past hedgerows that protected neatly plowed fields. A hill rose up before them, and on the crest of it stood a high limestone wall.

Yelling obscenities at the fox, Lord Burgess headed directly for the wall. He rose in his stirrups as he topped the barrier. "Now," he yelled. "Now I've got you!"

Sultan took the jump easily, as did Argos. Neck to neck, Patricia and Lord Longe galloped down the downward slope of the hill.

Behind them came the pound of hooves. They could hear Colonel Charteris's shouts as he approached the wall. Then, as he took the jump, the colonel lost his balance.

His yell caused Patricia to glance over her shoulder. She was in time to see the colonel pitch sideways out of his saddle. Missing the wall by inches, he thudded heavily to the ground and lay still.

Chapter Eight

The colonel was not the only one in trouble. His fall had unbalanced his horse, and the black gelding took his jump clumsily. Patricia cried out as the animal stumbled, fell, then slid helplessly down the hillside.

Freddy rode around the wall in time to see Lord Longe dismount and kneel beside the colonel. "Is he d-dead?" he asked.

Lord Longe's voice was dry. "Hardly."

He got to his feet as Captain Farell topped the wall and came cantering up. Dismounting, the young officer hurried up to his chief. "Sir, are you all right?" he cried.

The colonel twitched and groaned. In the same dry tone Lord Longe explained, "It's unwise to drink before a hunt."

"That worthless screw threw me," the colonel accused.

He sat up and glared down the incline. His gelding had managed to regain its feet. Patricia was on her knees examining its right foreleg.

Ignoring the colonel's sputterings, Lord Longe strode down the slope of the hill toward Patricia, who said, "There is something the matter with its right knee."

The duke's son ran his hand lightly over the beast's elbow and knee. Patricia watched him anxiously. "Is it broken?" she wondered.

"Useless bone setter." Leaning on his secretary's arm, the colonel was making his way down the hillside. He made a sorry picture. His hunt coat was covered with grass and splashed with mud, his hat had fallen off, and his cravat had come undone. His square face had a slightly greenish tinge to it as he growled, "To think that I paid three hundred guineas down for that worthless puffer."

Then he stopped complaining and scowled at Lord Longe. "Here, what's he doing with my horse?"

Patricia explained coldly, "Lord Longe is trying to determine whether its leg is broken."

The colonel snorted. "Any fool can see that it is. I'll have to shoot the miserable screw."

Lord Burgess, who had reluctantly doubled back to see what had befallen the colonel, nodded. "Yes, poor beast. Nothing for it but to put it out of its misery, hey?"

Lord Longe now said, "That mightn't be necessary. I can't be sure, but I believe that it's only a matter of a sprained tendon."

"Have you turned horse doctor now?" the colonel interrupted nastily. "But perhaps you're more concerned with beasts than you are about men."

Something flashed in the depths of Lord Longe's eyes. Patricia, seeing that deadly light, clenched

126

her fists. *Do it,* she wanted to cry. *Give him the thrashing he deserves.*

She watched hopefully as Lord Longe set down the gelding's foreleg and straightened to his full, powerful height. "You had better explain that remark, Charteris," he said.

The colonel looked around him for support but found none. Lord Burgess was contemplating the doomed horse and mournfully calculating its value. Captain Farell looked uneasy. Freddy, openly hostile, snapped, "I'd think you'd c-care about your own horse."

"You are beginning to try my patience, Charteris," Lord Longe continued.

Colonel Charteris blustered. "This is not the time or place." Then, when the duke's son began to move in on him, he mumbled, "I don't feel well."

"Coward!"

As the word burst from Patricia, Lord Longe stopped in his tracks. For an instant he felt himself go cold at the contempt in her voice, and then an uncontrollable anger burned through his veins. Charteris was the cause of his troubles, and today he would have satisfaction.

But even while he strode forward to lock his hands around Charteris's throat, the man turned tail and stumbled off behind the wall. About to give pursuit, Lord Longe found his way blocked by the captain.

"Get out of my way," the duke's son commanded.

But the captain held his ground. "Beg you'll let him alone for a moment," he explained. "He's busy being sick, don't you know."

Sounds from behind the wall attested to the truth of these words. "Not responsible for what he says—disguised, you see," Captain Farell added apologetically. "Realize it's bad form—but lady's present—no use pursuing the matter."

He nodded meaningfully toward Patricia, and after a few moments Lord Longe turned silently away.

Farell was right, he thought. It was worse than useless to try and change Patricia Surrey's mind. No matter what he said, no matter how she softened to him momentarily, she could never forgive him. Despair drove out even his anger until he heard the colonel's black gelding neigh.

That anguished sound recalled him to present reality. Almost wearily, the duke's son turned back to the condemned horse.

Patricia's heart ached as she saw the pain in Lord Longe's eyes. His face told her that there was little hope that the horse could be saved.

Meanwhile, the colonel was staggering around the wall. "I'm feeling unwell," he moaned. "Farell, shoot the beast, and we'll go on."

Patricia was horrified. "But Lord Longe has said that the bone may not be broken!" When the colonel ignored her, she rounded on her uncle. "Uncle Hector, please do not let him do this cruel thing."

Lord Burgess made unhappy noises in his throat. It went against his grain to destroy so fine a beast. At any other time he would have remonstrated with the colonel, but now he did not dare anger the man. He could only suggest feebly, "Perhaps you should have the horse doctor take a look. Hey? Can't do any harm."

Colonel Charteris looked sullen. "It's my horse, and I want it shot. Serves the cursed screw right for throwing me."

It was more than Patricia could bear. She confronted the colonel crying, "But it is all your fault. If you were not foxed, you would not have been lying beside that rasper. And your poor horse became unbalanced and hurt itself because of you. How can you murder it when there is a chance it can be saved?"

The colonel's eyes resembled popped green grapes. "Let me tell you, ma'am, that I'm not used to being lectured—"

"That is because you shout so loudly that you cannot hear anything but the sound of your own voice," Patricia interrupted.

Lord Longe spoke into the charged silence that followed. "You say you paid three hundred pounds for this horse. Very well, I offer you four."

Everyone stared at his lordship, and Lord Burgess expostulated, "But his leg's broke. It's no use buying an animal with a bum leg."

"Four hundred pounds." Then, as the colonel remained silent, Lord Longe added sardonically, "Are you trying to drive up the price?"

Lord Burgess leaned down to catch the colonel's arm. "Think about it," he urged. "Hey? Your horse's no good to you now. Knacker's meat. Let Longe have the horse. It won't do him any good."

Under cover of the muttered discussion that ensued, Patricia approached Lord Longe. In a low tone she asked, "Do you think that there is a chance that the horse can be saved?"

"I don't know."

His curtness surprised her until she saw how hard his eyes had become. She realized then that the colonel's horse was doomed. But rather than let a man like the colonel execute the animal, Lord

Longe was going to do it himself, with mercy and kindness.

Patricia's heart swelled, and she felt a knot forming in her throat. Lord Longe's gesture might be foolish, but she could not help honoring his decency.

"All right," the colonel agreed. "The useless beast's yours for four hundred pounds, and much good may it do you. How am I to be paid?"

Lord Longe's lip curled in distaste, but all he said was, "My man will bring the sum to you this evening."

"Well, I must s-say!" Freddy burst out. "I think you'd be ashamed t-to sell a useless horse."

"Oh, hold your tongue," growled Lord Burgess.

He had noted that the huntsman, the whippers-in, the earth-stoppers, and other menials were listening with great interest to their betters' brangling. "Stop gawking," he snarled at them. "The hunt's over. Hi, you," he added to one of the second horsemen, "give Colonel Charteris a horse, and let's get home."

Glumly, Lord Burgess watched the colonel clambering onto the borrowed horse. He had just realized that Charteris was a dashed poor sort of fellow. He had allowed himself to be unseated in a hunt and had ruined his gelding in the process. Clearly the man had no bottom.

But he was also as rich as Golden Ball. Lord Burgess winced as he considered his forthcoming interview with his wife. He had put it off as long as he could and had hoped to have one last good hunt before the ax fell.

And that crafty old dog fox was probably watching and laughing at them all. A fine hunt it had been, thought the baronet dismally.

Pasting a smile on his lips, he invited the colonel to Burgess Hall for a little luncheon. The colonel agreed, first ordering his secretary to go home and await his return.

Captain Farell looked particularly wooden as he saluted his chief. He remained at attention until Lord Burgess and the colonel had ridden away. Then, making an abrupt about-face, he spoke to Lord Longe.

"If you require assistance," he began, then flushed at his lordship's look of astonishment. "Taking Jet back to Riverway, I mean—glad to help."

Lord Longe shook his head. "I'm obliged to you, but I mean to send for my groom and a cart. The less the animal—his name's Jet, is it?—is moved, the better."

"One of our people can ride Riverway and fetch your groom," Freddy suggested eagerly. "I'll arrange it, sh-shall I?"

As he went trotting off, Patricia saw that the look of pain had returned to Lord Longe's eyes.

Her own eyes filled with tears, and she whispered, "It is as I feared. You really do not think you can help Jet."

"I'm going to try."

It was afternoon by the time Patricia and Freddy returned to Burgess Hall, and Charms announced that my lord, my lady, and Colonel Charteris had gone in to luncheon. Would Mr. Harmon and Miss Surrey be joining them?

Freddy made a face and retreated out of doors.

Patricia declined. Her usually healthy appetite had vanished at the thought of what might happen to Jet, and she had no desire to see the colonel. Apparently she was not alone in this, for as she climbed the stairs to her room, she heard Delphie's petulant voice.

"I will not go downstairs, Wiggy." There was a distressed murmur from the governess. "No, I do not care what you say. I will *not* go downstairs and watch that blockhead stuff himself."

The boom of Charteris's laughter pursued Patricia into her chamber. As she unfastened her shako, she considered that Colonel Charteris was a despicable man. No matter what Lord Longe had done on the Peninsula, he had acted like a gentleman today, and the colonel had been the one to play craven.

The thought that Lord Longe might have already put Jet out of his pain made Patricia so unhappy that she did not even have the energy to change out of her riding dress. She sat down in a chair by her window and gazed out across the downs, seeing nothing and thinking of nothing but of Jet and the anger and pain she had felt when the healthy young horse was condemned to death. How strange that of everyone present at the hunt, only Lord Jonathan Longe had completely shared her feelings.

She did not know how long she remained seated by the window, but she was roused sometime later by the colonel's boisterous farewells. Patricia was grateful when she heard him ride away. Now, she must make an effort and change—

A blood-curdling shriek shattered Patricia's thoughts. Horrified, she jumped to her feet and ran out onto the landing where she met Delphie and

132

Miss Wigge. "What on earth is happening?" the governess was twittering. "What cataclysm has befallen us?"

As if in answer, Freddy came hurrying upstairs. "I wouldn't go down there if I was you," he warned. "The pater and M-Mama are having it out in the morning room."

Lord Burgess's petulant voice could now be heard expostulating, "I tell you, Maria, there's no use trying to eat me. Hey? No help for it—"

Another shriek disrupted this speech. Shaking his head gloomily, Freddy walked off in the direction of his room. Miss Wigge, looking scared, began to quote Shakespeare.

Patricia felt stifled. She needed to leave the house and everybody in it. Returning to her room, she snatched up her shako and crammed it on her head. Then, picking up her riding crop, she started down the stairs. As she passed the morning room, she heard her uncle exclaim, "Talking won't mend fences. Hey? It's done, I tell you. You'll gain nothing by raking coals over my head."

Lady Burgess's answering wail sent Patricia out of the door at a run. She did not slacken speed until she reached the stables where Seamus eyed her in astonishment.

"Going where this time, Miss Patricia?" he wondered.

"That," Patricia replied, "is not your business."

The groom seemed to swell. "Not my business, is it, now?" he demanded. "Argos, am I hearing right? When herself's sainted lady mother's begged me with tears in her eyes to have the care of Miss Patricia along of her horse?"

With an effort Patricia restrained herself. "I am

sorry. I am in a black mood and—I am *very* sorry, Seamus, so do stop lecturing Argos in that horrid way. I need to get out of the house for a while, that is all. I do not know where I want to ride."

"Why couldn't you be telling me so from the first? I'll saddle up and follow you."

Patricia protested, but Seamus would have none of it. If Miss Patricia was set on junketing around the county in the late afternoon, he informed Argos sternly, she would not go unchaperoned. If herself had forgotten the laws of propriety, there were some that had not.

Luckily Patricia's sense of humor returned during her groom's speech. Everything that had happened today was so dreadful that it was almost funny. Then she thought of poor Jet, and she wanted to cry.

Suddenly she knew where she must ride. Silently she guided Argos over the rolling downs, and when they came to the fork in the road, she turned east.

"So that's where we're going," Seamus commented, "to see that poor, hurt beast that Mr. Harmon told me about, is it? Arrah, but it's a fine, fair place Riverway is."

It was indeed. The Leads River shimmered like a golden ribbon in the late afternoon sun. Primroses and dandelions bloomed among the mossy stones that lay near the road. There was a flash of yellow as a goldfinch sped into the shelter of the fine old oaks that boardered Lord Longe's estate.

Even in her troubled state of mind, Patricia could feel the beauty and the sense of peace that filled Riverway Place. This mood continued as she rode into the courtyard, where Owens came tramping out to take her bridle.

It had not been long since Patricia last saw him, but the change in the old fellow was truly amazing. He looked neat, and his white hair had been trimmed. He appeared much happier, even fatter, and his crumpled face split in a grin when he saw Patricia.

Respectfully he tugged his forelock to her. "Looking fer the guv'nor, Missie? 'E's in the stable wi' the 'urt 'orse."

Then Jet had not been destroyed. Joy and relief flooded Patricia, but before she could question Owens further, there was a roar from the stables.

"Not that way," Lord Longe's voice was heard to shout. "The harness must be padded with sheepskin, first, or the leather will cut into his belly. Damnation! Do I have to think of everything?"

Seamus looked scandalized at such language, but before he could say anything Patricia ordered, "Seamus, stay here, please."

She was out of her saddle before he could dismount and on her way to the stable. Here the first thing she noticed was Jet. The horse was being urged forward to stand across a leather harness that had been suspended from the ceiling by two wooden blocks and tackles. In spite of the efforts of the groom that held him, the horse whinnied and balked.

"Wait, Heeming, he's too frightened." Patricia saw that Lord Longe was kneeling on the stable floor, where he'd been engaged in arranging a thick, soft sheepskin over the harness. He had thrown off his coat and waistcoat and his shirtsleeves had been rolled back over muscular forearms. "Let me try. The rest of you be still."

In the ensuing silence Patricia looked about her.

The stable was large, well appointed, and spotless with spacious stalls and a floor that sloped down toward the center drains. From their stalls many fine horses whickered sympathy for Jet.

"Softly friend, easily." Murmuring soothing words, Lord Longe took Jet's bridle and coaxed him forward. He held him steady as the harness was fitted under his belly.

"Tha's done it, master," the groom called Heeming exclaimed. 'Up wi' him, now, lads. Put your backs into it, wilta?"

Sweating grooms began to work the blocks and tackles. Jet whinnied in fear as he felt himself rising a few inches up into the air, and Heeming exclaimed, "He's never going to stay there, master. Happen he'll do himself a mischief."

"I'll quieten him. Take everyone out, now, but stay close yourself. I may need your help."

Heeming left, sweeping his helpers before him. As he neared the door, he saw Patricia and sent her a startled look. When she laid a finger on her lips and shook her head, he went out silently and closed the stable door behind him.

Suddenly Lord Longe looked up. "I thought I told you all to leave—" he began, then exclaimed in astonishment. "You!"

She stammered, "I did not mean to intrude. I merely came to see how Jet was—"

"I'm delighted that you have come."

The welcome in his voice was unfeigned. It gladdened her, but she felt flustered, too. "I could not be easy until I learned about Jet's leg," she explained. "It is not broken after all?"

"Heeming feels sure that it is not."

Lord Longe spoke almost automatically. He could

not believe that Patricia had come to Riverway. She had called him "coward" this morning, and yet, when he searched her face, he could see no sign of contempt. All he could read in her eyes was concern for the horse.

He gazed at her so intently that Patricia's confusion increased. She pretended to examine the blocks and tackles saying, "The idea of putting him in a harness is very clever. Was it you who thought of it?"

"It's a trick I learned on the—along the way."

He had meant to say, "on the Continent," Patricia knew. As the familiar ghosts of Talavera seemed to darken the stable, she realized that she had made a grave error in judgment. It would have been enough to send Seamus to inquire about the horse.

Why had she come? Patricia glanced out of the corners of her eyes at Lord Longe and saw that he had stepped forward to examine Jet's harness. The sheepskin padding that prevented the leather from cutting into Jet's belly had shifted.

"May I enlist your aid for a moment?" Lord Longe asked. "I'd call Heeming, but I don't want to excite the horse again. If I lower him, will you readjust the padding?"

Willingly Patricia went up to the black gelding and soothed it. But as Lord Longe worked one of the blocks and tackles, her attention shifted. Jack had once remarked that a person's hands showed a great deal about his character, and Lord Longe's hands were strong and self-assured, yet gentle. In spite of what people said about him, Patricia thought, these were trustworthy hands.

She averted her eyes from his lordship, who was

also having trouble concentrating on his task. He was very much aware of Patricia's nearness and of the fragrance of roses that she wore. He was fascinated by the way her honey-gold hair curls parted at the nape of her neck.

Lord Longe wanted desperately to kiss that delicate white neck.

In silence he watched Patricia adjust the sheepskin padding and then worked the block and tackle until Jet was suspended as before and realized that she was looking anxious. "Are you aware that both Jet's forelegs are showing red?" she asked.

"Yes. That happened in the fall. I was going to foment the lacerations as soon as I got the weight off that foreleg."

Patricia went down on her knees to examine Jet's hurts. It seemed natural under the circumstances for Lord Longe to come and kneel beside her, but the effect of his nearness was alarming. Patricia glanced uneasily toward the closed stable door.

Lord Longe followed the direction of her gaze. He could feel her discomfort and knew that in a moment she would be gone.

And he could not bear to let her go so soon. "Perhaps I can ask another favor," he said. "Jet might become restive while I apply the poultice. If you could talk to him as you did before, it would make my task much easier."

"Your groom is awaiting your orders," she reminded him.

"But Jet trusts you and is easy with you."

Patricia hesitated. Her instincts told her that she must go at once. "My aunt and uncle keep country hours," she hedged.

She was rising to her feet when he shrugged. "Oh, certainly. I must not keep you from your dinner, Miss Surrey."

He made it sound as though she were being selfish. Patricia frowned.

"Very well," she agreed. "I will stay and help you."

As Lord Longe went about readying the poultice, he could hardly fix his mind on what he was doing. He, who had calmly faced cannon fire and had stood with a tattered remnant of his men against the charge of Napoleon's fearsome cavalry, actually felt weak in the knees.

"It is an ugly scrape," Patricia murmured.

She looked up as he bent down, and her fragrant hair brushed his cheek. Lord Longe felt lightheaded. With a heroic effort, he managed to keep his hand steady.

"It was an ugly fall," he pointed out.

"And Colonel Charteris dared to blame his poor horse." Patricia's hazel eyes narrowed. "I am not sorry that I called him a coward. I only wish I had boxed his ears."

Lord Longe stopped in the act of securing the poultice to Jet's legs. She had called *Charteris* a coward. He had misunderstood everything. Exultation roared through him.

"I didn't understand." He had spoken more to himself than to her, but she turned her head and looked at him inquiringly.

There was an instant when the world seemed to be holding its breath. Patricia saw the change in Lord Longe's face, and somewhere deep in her brain an alarm began to clamor. It ordered her to leap to her feet and run to the door, *to go now.*

Hardly realizing what she did, Patricia got up. So did Lord Longe. Then, before either of them had a chance to think, he swept her into his arms and kissed her.

Patricia felt herself disintegrating. Her bones seemed to have withdrawn their support, and she was forced to cling to Lord Longe. Very obligingly he held her close to him while his lips caressed hers in a wondrous, exciting way.

Jonathan, Patricia thought rapturously. *Oh, Jonathan.*

Lord Longe wasn't thinking at all. Joy that was almost madness filled him. He was dimly aware that Patricia was in his arms, that she was not pushing him away, that she was actually kissing him back.

"Patricia," he whispered, "my dear lo—"

He broke off in midword, for just as swiftly as it had come, his madness left him, and Lord Longe realized just what he was doing.

Even if Patricia loathed the colonel, Charteris's lies had not been laid to rest. Talavera still stood like a drawn sword between them. Until Charteris admitted those lies publically, there could be no real trust or love.

Very reluctantly Lord Longe dropped his arms from around Patricia and looked down into her face. Her cheeks were rosy, her mouth soft with invitation. Her eyelashes were dark curves on her cheeks for a moment before she opened her eyes and regarded him.

Every word he knew deserted Lord Longe. He stood tongue-tied as realization and horror filled Patricia's eyes. The best he could do was to stammer, "I beg your pardon. I don't know how—the excitement of the moment—"

In another minute he would sound just like Farell. Lord Longe felt like ten species of idiot as Patricia squared her shoulders and raised her chin.

"Pray do not r-regard it," she said coldly.

Patricia despised herself for the hen-hearted quaver in her voice. She loathed herself even more for what had happened during the last few seconds. She still couldn't believe that she had allowed Lord Longe to kiss her.

And she had kissed him back! Patricia lashed herself with every hard name she could think of. Aloud she said, "I am returning to Burgess Hall."

She tried to speak with becoming hauteur, but Lord Longe was aware of the quaver in her tone. His heart ached with love for her. He wanted nothing more than to sweep her back into his arms and tell her what was in his heart. He wanted to tell her the truth about Talavera.

But common sense checked him. He still didn't know the complete truth about the battle, but the pieces of the puzzle had just begun to fit, and to rush things now might prove disastrous.

Lord Longe clasped his hands behind his back. "Thank you for your concern about Jet," he told her.

He was trying to be formal, but he didn't succeed. His deep voice shivered through her like music. It invited her back into his arms. Almost, Patricia took a step forward—but this time sanity intervened in time.

Abandoning all pretense of dignity, Patricia lifted her skirts and practically ran out of the stable. Outside, she told Seamus that they were leaving immediately.

The groom had been gossiping with Owens and a few of Lord Longe's grooms. As they rode away from Riverway he said, "That groom, Heeming, was after telling me what Lord Longe did with the harness. A very knowing man, his lordship."

Patricia felt her cheeks burn.

"Him and Owens were both in the war," Seamus went on. "Owens said he served under Colonel Charteris."

Patricia slowed Argos so that Seamus could draw up to her. "But the colonel almost horsewhipped him!"

Seamus pursed his lips. "Some officers mistreat their men. Not like Lord Longe, I'm thinking. According to Heeming, his lordship's a gallant officer."

"It is not like you to gossip, Seamus," Patricia interrupted. "What Lord Longe does or does not do is no concern of yours—or mine."

Seamus dropped back to ride behind his mistress once more. From this position he continued, "Lord Longe, the colonel, and Owens were all together at Talavera. But you wouldn't want to be knowing what else Owens told me at all, at all. 'Twould be gossip."

With difficulty, Patricia held her tongue. "Aye, Argos, I could tell a tale," her groom continued. "I could say that according to Heeming, there wasn't a man who served under Lord Longe that wouldn't have been cut into little pieces for his lordship."

The Nineteenth Foot Guard *had* been cut to pieces. The regiment had suffered grievously because of the duke's son. She had sworn to hate him forever, and instead—

Patricia slammed her heels into Argos's side and sent him galloping homeward. But as swiftly as she rode, she couldn't forget Lord Longshanks's kisses.

Chapter Nine

Candles were being lit by the time Patricia reached Burgess Hall, but the family had not yet sat down to dine. There seemed to be undercurrents of uneasiness in the old Tudor mansion, and the servants looked nervous and uncertain. When Patricia went upstairs, her cousins were waiting to pounce on her.

"It's happened," Freddy began ominously. "There was a huge dustup between M-Mama and the pater. He's finally told her about his d-debts."

Patricia recalled that she had heard a part of that altercation. It seemed to have happened long ago. Ever since she had kissed Lord Longshanks, time itself had gone askew.

"No need to look so unhappy, Pat," Freddy said kindly. "The pater's always in and out of dun territory. S-somehow, he always comes up to scratch."

Delphie said tragically, "That is all very well for *you* to say. You have not been longing for the Sea-

144

son. My come-out will be canceled, and Mama will make all of us economize, and Papa will be cross. You cannot realize how horrid it will be."

Miss Wigge, hovering in the background, had for once no quotation to offer. She was considering Lady Burgess's future economies and worrying about her position. Miss Delphinium was nearly eighteen, after all, and did not need a governess any longer.

"Perhaps," she ventured, "it will not come to that. Dear Lord Burgess may yet recoup his losses."

"Don't see how," Freddy said, then fell silent as a liveried footman, holding the five-branched candelabra that would light the family down to dinner, ascended the stairs. "Might as well go down," he went on, "though it ain't going to be a p-pleasant meal."

Patricia went upstairs to wash and change and some ten minutes later entered the small dining room where the Burgesses always ate when *en famille*. This chamber was tonight as dismal as a tomb. Neither a roaring fire nor cheerful candlelight could lighten the morose features of Lord Burgess or warm his lady's fulminating countenance. They sat stiffly across from each other in painful silence while their children and Miss Wigge kept their eyes on their plates.

Lord Burgess glanced up as Patricia came into the room and grumbled, "You're late."

"I went riding and forgot the time," she apologized.

"There will be no more riding done at Burgess Hall," Lady Burgess cast her spouse a darkling look. "You might as well realize that because of Lord Burgess all the horses are to be sold."

Freddy started as though stung by a wasp. "S-sold?"

"Your papa," Lady Burgess continued witheringly, "is selling the horses to pay a portion of his debts." She ignored her husband's wild motions toward a footman who had just entered the room with a soup tureen and added, "I collect that it will not end there. All will be sacrificed. *All.*"

"Oh, for God's sake," Lord Burgess growled. "Don't start in again, Maria."

"I hope, *my lord,*" his wife continued in a sepulchral voice, "that you will be the one to inform the servants that they are on notice."

The footman dropped the tureen. Soup splattered on Lord Burgess, who hopped up from his chair exclaiming, "Of all the clumsy—hey? Get out, you nincompoop, and clean up this mess later." As the incoherent footman made his escape he added angrily, "Must you brangle in front of the servants, Maria? You know how their jaws will wag belowstairs."

His lady icily reminded him that it was not she who had "brought disgrace down upon them all." It was obviously a turn of phrase that had been used before. Freddy shot a meaningful look at Delphie, who rolled her eyes. Only Miss Wigge looked properly subdued.

"Any man can have bad luck," Lord Burgess protested. "Damn, Maria, it's not so bad. Putting my cattle under the hammer will satisfy the jackals."

"Your daughter's come-out will be canceled. Naturally," his lady continued coldly, "you have not thought of that disgrace. And have you considered where we shall live in London now that our town house has been sold?"

Delphie uttered a wail. "Our London house, sold! Oh, how could you, Papa? And my come-out canceled—"

"No need to take on so," Lord Burgess interrupted hastily. "You don't need a come-out. Hey? Charteris has offered for you." He paused to let this news sink in then added with somewhat forced heartiness, "He meant to have a word with you today, but you didn't come downstairs, so he spoke to me. It's all right and tight and as it should be."

"It is not!" Delphie bounced to her feet crying, "I absolutely will not marry Colonel Charteris!"

Her father's mouth hung open. Her mother gasped, "Delphinium, compose yourself. Though I must own that your papa could have used more tact in announcing the colonel's offer, it is not one to be despised."

"I despise *him*," Delphie shouted. "I have only endured him because of Captain Farell."

"You'll marry Charteris if I say so, and that's an end to it."

Lord Burgess glared at Delphie, who announced defiantly, "When I marry, I shall marry for love."

" 'Love conquers all, let us, too, give in to love,' " Miss Wigge quoted feebly.

"You are a fool, ma'am. Be pleased to hold your tongue. As to you, Delphinium," Lord Burgess continued sternly, "go to your room and stay there. I'll deal with you later."

Miss Wigge, looking both scared and hungry, rose to her feet. Delphie flounced off and would have made an inspired exit had she not run into the footman who had been listening with his ear to the keyhole.

"Get rid of the pack of them." Lord Burgess

147

growled, when the door was shut again. "Those servants eat me out of house and home and are no bloody use to anyone." Lady Burgess sniffed. "Ay, madam, it's all very well for you to fly into the boughs with me, but consider the facts. Hey? If Charteris walks into parson's mousetrap with Delphie, we'll be in clover again. If not, we'll all be up the River Tick."

Much as she hated to agree with her spouse, Lady Burgess knew that he was right. "I will speak to her," she promised.

Patricia had been listening in mounting horror. "This is beyond all belief," she exclaimed. "Uncle Hector, you know what kind of creature the colonel is. How can you expect Delphie to marry him?"

Lord Burgess had had a trying day. First, there had been that disastrous hunt, and then there had been the scene with his wife. For a woman whose whole life was given to the correct use of etiquette, the baronet thought sourly, Maria had a tongue that could put the Royal Navy to shame.

Still smarting from the memory of his wife's references to his complete lack of character, his total want of wit, and his utter disregard of his duties as head of the family, he rounded on his niece. "Haven't you done enough?" he demanded.

Patricia replied coldly that she did not know what he meant.

"As if you didn't know. You were rude to Charteris this afternoon. Hey? Actually called him a fool."

"He *acted* like a f-fool," Freddy began.

"I'm used to my son being the village idiot," the baronet interrupted rudely, "but I thought that you

148

had more sense, Patricia. Siding with Longe about a useless horse with a broken leg."

His niece's eyes flashed at the memory. "The horse is not useless. It's leg is *not* broken, and it is going to recover."

"How would you know that unless—d'you mean to tell me that you went to Riverway yourself?"

Defiantly Patricia nodded. Freddy looked impressed, but Lady Burgess placed a hand on her heart. "How imprudent, my dear," she exclaimed faintly. "What will people say of such forward conduct? If Lady Were had seen you, I should never hear the end of it."

About to retort that her visit to Riverway had been unexceptional, Patricia remembered just how improper it had been. Her cheeks felt warm, but she insisted, "I do not care a rush what anyone says. Seamus was with me—"

"I don't care if Prinny himself was with you," Lord Burgess shouted. "Hey? You'll not have anything more to do with that fellow. No one in this family is to speak with him again."

"I will speak with whomever I like, Uncle Hector."

The words were out before Patricia had time to think. She felt almost as astonished as her uncle, who turned very red and declared, "While you are under my roof, you'll do as I say."

He thumped his fist on the table and glared at his niece. Patricia rose to her feet and spoke with icy dignity. "You make yourself clear, sir. I will arrange to remove to Somerset at once."

Lady Burgess uttered a faint shriek. "Dear Patricia, pray compose yourself. You cannot return to

Somerset and live alone while Jack is abroad. Hector, pray reason with her. How would it *look*?"

"It'd look a d-dashed sight better than cutting Lord Longe." Valiantly Freddy cast himself into the breach. "I agree with Pat. Colonel Charteris is a dashed b-bounder, and my sister shouldn't have to marry him."

Lord Burgess attempted to quell his offspring with a glare, but Freddy stood his ground. Faced with this unexpected mutiny, the baronet threw his plump hands to heaven and demanded to know why he had been plagued with such a sheep-witted family.

He then added, "Now listen to me, all of you. If that fellow shows his face here, I'll have him thrown out. And I don't care a damned haypenny if his father's the emperor of China, either."

"As to you," he added to Freddy, "there'll be no more cavorting around the county with Longe. If you put one step out of this house, I'll take my whip to you."

Unable to trust her temper, Patricia rose and left the dining room. She was barely outside when Freddy caught up to her.

He was fuming. "If this ain't a mare's n-nest, I don't know what is. We can't let Lord Longe be turned off the property like a—a common tradesman. I'd die of s-shame." He caught his cousin's arm to add, "You must warn him, Pat."

"I!"

Freddy cast a speaking glance at the first floor landing, where the burly figure of Mimsby could be seen lurking. "He's been eavesdropping, like as not," Freddy continued sourly. "And anyway, the pater's s-sure to have *him* watch me, ain't he? Precious chance I'd have of getting away from that squeeze-crab. But you could go."

"I cannot," Patricia whispered.

Freddy frowned at the anguish in her face. "You're the last one I'd have expected to turn m-missish. S-since when have you worried about a lot of s-stuffy rules?"

Since I kissed Lord Longshanks, Patricia thought. Aloud, she said, "There are rules and rules, Freddy."

"At least we could send Seamus with a note," Freddy urged. "You c-can warn him about the pater and leave it up to him."

But Patricia still resisted. "The note should come from you. Uncle Hector is your father, after all."

Freddy sighed. "D-don't remind me. Oh, very well, I'll write the plaguey thing. Where's p-paper and a pen?"

After considerable effort the note was written. Seamus left on his mission early in the morning and returned some time later full of news.

"Arrah, it's doing fine is that poor horse," he told his mistress. "The harness is working like a charm, and the sprained foreleg is healing clean. Sure and his lordship was right about that, Miss Patricia."

"I'm glad to hear it." In a carefully casual tone Patricia inquired, "So you delivered the note to Lord Longe?"

"I didn't deliver it *to* his lordship because he weren't there. Himself and that old boyo, Owens, left Riverway early this morning. For Scotland, I was told."

Astonished for a moment, Patricia realized what had happened. Lord Longe had obviously realized how much that scene in the stables had disturbed her and had gone away rather than embarrass her. Though grateful for his lordship's discretion, Patricia wondered if the odd, squeezing sensation around her heart was caused by relief—or by regret.

Regret that Lord Longshanks had gone away? Impossible. Yet, as she turned back toward the house, Patricia could not shake off an inexplicable sense of loss.

Days of unpleasantness followed. At Burgess Hall the baronet's stable was sacrificed to satisfy his most pressing creditors. Lord Burgess had drawn the line at putting his own steed under the hammer, but he watched glumly as his precious hunters, the matched bays that had drawn his phaeton, the carriage horses, his son's gelding, and his wife's and daughter's mares were sold off.

Gladly would he have sold his property instead of his beloved horses, but Burgess Hall was entailed, his other properties mortgaged to the hilt, and the London town house was gone. And for the moment Lord Burgess lacked the courage to sell his wife's jewels or the family plate.

The baronet's only consolation was that this state of affairs was temporary. As soon as Charteris was betrothed to Delphie, Lord Burgess could borrow on the credit of his wealthy future son-in-law. Then, he promised himself, his stables would once again resound to the neighs of blood horses. Meanwhile he could take no chances. Lord Longe must come no more to Burgess Hall, and as to his daughter, she would knuckle under as all females should.

But Delphie proved a problem. She absolutely and categorically refused to see or have anything to do with the colonel. Reasoning with her did no good, nor did threats. Delphie tossed her pretty head and remained as stubborn as a goat.

"What pisses my goose is that we may lose Charteris yet," Lord Burgess fumed to his wife one afternoon. "We must do something, Maria, to sweeten things up, or he may give up in disgust. We must plan a 'beau geste,' as the Frenchies put it."

"What have you in mind?" When told, her ladyship wrinkled her nose, an affectation that made her look more like an anxious rabbit than ever. "But a ball in the colonel's honor would be most expensive. The cost of the flowers alone—"

"Oh, hang the expense," Lord Burgess exclaimed. "The end justifies the means. Hey? Once Charteris is shackled to Delphie, we won't have to worry about money. We can go on as we did before."

On the point of making an acid rejoinder about her spouse's gaming habits, Lady Burgess remembered some diamond earrings that she had been wanting. They were the very thing for an important occasion like a ball and would impress even Lady Were.

"Very well," she sighed. "If you say that a ball must be given, it shall be given. But Delphinium will need a new ball gown. I daresay that *I* may contrive to make do with the old rags I possess."

"Old rags, nothing, you've got closetfuls of clothes. But look, Maria," the baronet continued earnestly, "Soften Delphie up with some gewgaws and a pretty gown and bring her around. We need to announce her engagement at the ball. Once the Season begins, Charteris will very likely be hooked by some other pretty face or a fat fortune."

Lady Burgess flung herself into preparations with

a will. Within a scant week a prestigious London caterer had been engaged, an orchestra selected, and invitations penned by her ladyship's secretary to persons of consequence begging their presence at a ball in honor of Colonel Waldo Charteris.

One of the first acceptances to the ball came from the guest of honor himself. A few days after the invitations were sent out, Captain Farell delivered his superior officer's note of acceptance to Lady Burgess.

She smiled as she read his note and said, "Pray convey our pleasure to the dear colonel and say that we will look forward to seeing him."

The handsome young officer bowed, and Lady Burgess congratulated herself for not having invited him to the ball. After Delphinium's dinner-table declaration, she had taken pains not to let Captain Farell get anywhere near her idiotish daughter.

"I am sure, Captain, that you are anxious to return to your duties, so I shall not detain you," my lady continued. She added significantly, "How sad that you will miss my daughter, who has no doubt some message of her own to send the dear colonel. She is visiting Mrs. Yancey this afternoon and will be gone for several hours."

The captain saluted with a jerk that nearly snapped his spine, turned on his heel, and strode out of the door.

"Blockhead," Lady Burgess murmured.

In the hallway the blockhead halted. "Miss Harmon away," he muttered distractedly. "Oh, Delphinium, my love. No—mustn't think of her like that—forbidden fruit."

"Captain Farell?"

The young officer whirled about so suddenly that he collided with a hat rack. "M-Miss Surrey," he stammered. "Didn't hear you—mean to say—occupied with my thoughts, don't you know."

"I heard you speaking to yourself," Patricia explained. "Are you committing some new poem to memory?"

The captain shuddered. "God, no. Mean to say—beg your pardon—not the right thing to say to a female—good day, Miss Surrey."

But no sooner had she passed him by when he exclaimed, "Miss Surrey—may I have a word? In private—yes, private, don't you know—what I have to say is—is of a nature that is—"

"Private?" she suggested.

He beamed. "Just the word I was looking for."

"In the yellow saloon, perhaps?"

Patricia gestured across the hall. The captain allowed her to lead the way into this small chamber then turned abruptly to face her. "Very good of you," he said. "Very kind. Need to talk to someone—Miss Harmon isn't at home today."

Patricia shook her head.

"Hoped to see her. Hoped to tell her—" he broke off and drew from his breast a bedraggled weed. "Miss Harmon gave this to me."

With some difficulty Patricia identified the weed as a daisy without petals.

"I treasure it. She picked it with her own hands." Somewhat incoherently the captain continued, "We had a moment together some time ago—colonel talking to Lord Burgess in the garden—we walked a distance apart—she picked this daisy and tore off the petals saying, 'I love him, I love him not, I love him—' "

"I know the custom," Patricia interrupted.

"She ended with, 'I love him,' " the captain concluded. "She gave me hope, Miss Surrey, that she was not altogether indifferent to me."

Not knowing what to say, Patricia was silent.

"I felt sometimes—Miss Harmon toying with me. No use taking me seriously, don't you know," he added dejectedly. "Good name, honorable, but no prospects to speak of—military career ahead of me, but not wealthy man—only a comfortable living left to me by late mother—not much by Lord Burgess's standards."

"I do not believe that my cousin is trifling with you," Patricia said gently. "She is young and can be thoughtless sometimes, but she would not hurt anyone for the world."

Captain Farell ran an agitated hand through his hair. "Want to think so, ma'am—fact is, not sure— for her sake learned the lute. Cursed awkward instrument, the lute. For her sake, wrote poetry— dashed wretched stuff," the captain added frankly, "brought me to the blush. Assure you—'Moon, June, bloom—' awful."

Patricia, who had heard several of the captain's efforts, silently agreed.

"Can't see why Miss Harmon likes that drivel— up to me, chuck it all into the fire." The captain chewed his lower lip for a moment before continuing, "For her sake—she wanted 'atmosphere', don't you know—I dressed up like a confounded gypsy. Then, nothing would please her but I should get myself up to look like Romeo. Must confess, Miss Surrey—felt like a fool."

No wonder the poor young man thought that Delphie was laughing at him. "Then why do any of it?" Patricia wondered.

Captain Farell said simply, "I love her."

Patricia was moved. Ludicrous though he might appear to others, the young officer was sincere. He loved Delphie with all his heart and soul.

An unaccountable ache filled her chest. To counter it, Patricia said, "I am persuaded that my cousin holds you in great esteem."

He caught her hand and wrung it in a painfully hard grip. "Very good—very kind—command me in anything, Miss Surrey. But it's hopeless, don't you know. Colonel Charteris—my superior officer—has offered for Miss Harmon. Lord Burgess plans to announce engagement at the ball. The colonel told me so—bragged, in fact."

"Oh, *base*," Patricia exclaimed.

"Should not say this to a lady—hang it, will say it anyway. Colonel Charteris is not a fit husband for Miss Harmon." The captain paused, lowered his voice and whispered, "Drinks."

"I should not have guessed it."

He did not seem to notice her satiric tone. "Not a thing that a lady would notice, don't you know, but lately, it's become worse. Since the incident at the hunt—drinks like a fish. Angry at Lord Longe for making him look like a fool. Dash it," the captain added earnestly, "he *did* look like a fool. By contrast, Lord Longe acted like a—a gentleman."

Patricia was silent, remembering.

Captain Farell continued, "Lord Longe acted badly at Talavera—there's no getting around that. But," he added fair mindedly, "I haven't seen him commit a craven act since I've met him. Fact is, acted a man's part in saving young Harmon from injury. And there was all that about the black gelding."

"He also kept Mr. Owens from a beating," Patricia mused.

"Don't know about Owens—looks like a perfect scoundrel to me—not the point anyway. Point is the colonel's not a fit husband for any young female."

Patricia understood that the captain was disillusioned with his employer and thus had softened toward the one man who continued to make Charteris look like a fool.

She was silent as the young officer continued, "If the colonel had accused Lord Longe face to face, it'd be one thing. Honorable, don't you know. Longe issues cartel—Colonel Charteris accepts—duel fought—one of them blows a hole through the other. Accepted way of gentlemen. But all this talking behind the back—too much like sneaking." He shook his head and repeated, "Not the kind of man to marry Miss Harmon."

Suddenly he seized Patricia's hand. "Will you help me, ma'am? I must see her before it's too late."

Though she sympathized with the captain, Patricia hesitated. She knew that Delphie could not possibly marry without her parents' consent. For Farell to meet her now would only bring more sorrow to them both.

"I must talk to her without all that da—confounded poetry," Captain Farell was saying. "Must talk to her heart to heart, don't you know. I beg you, Miss Surrey, arrange a meeting."

Throwing logic to the winds, Patricia capitulated. "Very well. I will do what I can—as long as I act as your chaperon."

He lifted her hand and dropped an awkwardly

fervent kiss on her knuckles. "Very good of you—your servant, ma'am—never forget your kindness."

Telling the captain that she would send him a message when the meeting could be arranged, Patricia sent him on his way. That evening, she spoke to Delphie and repeated all that the captain had said. "How do you feel about him, Delphie?" she then asked.

She had fully expected her cousin to go into romantic raptures. Instead Delphie said rather simply, "I am in love with him. My heart flutters when he is near."

Was a fluttering heart all there was to love? Patricia did not know she had asked the question aloud until her cousin said defensively, "You do not know what it is to love, Patricia."

Gray eyes the color of a summer dawn, a smile that could bring laughter or tug at the heart—and one kiss that had turned her world upside down. "No," Patricia said quietly, "it is plain that I do not."

Delphie hugged her. "I did not mean to sound cross," she said contritely. "I am only tired of being scolded by Papa and teased by Mama because I do not wish to marry the colonel. Mama says my betrothal is to be announced at the ball and insists that I do my duty to the family. Please, dearest, dearest Patricia, arrange a meeting between Arthur and me?"

Patricia sent a note to Captain Farell. Seamus, who carried the message, brought back the young secretary's jubilant thanks.

"But," he pointed out, "I'm bound to warn you, Miss Patricia. Lovers' meetings spell nothing but trouble."

Patricia lifted her brows at him. "You sound as though you have some experience in such matters."

The groom rubbed his nose gloomily. "I have that. Wasn't it myself who set up the tryst between Gerta, the miller's daughter, and Perkins, who was then my under groom in Somerset? And weren't they married as soon as the banns could be read? And didn't Gerta blame me forever after for having saddled her with a worthless husband? Holy saints preserve me from sweethearts."

It felt good to laugh. Patricia's mirth died, however, when Seamus warned, "And here's another thing. That colonel is someone I would not want as my enemy. Be careful, Miss Patricia."

"I can deal with Colonel Charteris."

Patricia spoke firmly, yet she felt uneasy as she returned to the house. She felt trouble prickling under her skin, and she wondered if she should cancel the rendezvous. Still, she had given her word.

The meeting took place next day. On pretext of delivering flowers from the colonel, Captain Farell arrived in the early afternoon. He had left the colonel snoring over his cups, Lady Burgess was closeted with the caterer, and Lord Burgess was recuperating from a late night of cards with his friends. No one was there to stop the captain from striding down the garden path toward the rose garden.

Behind the high hawthorn hedge, Patricia, Delphie, and Miss Wigge were waiting, but the captain had eyes for only his beloved. Dressed in blue sprigged muslin with a flat hat covered with cornflowers and daisies, Delphie looked adorable. When she held out her hands to him, the young man ran forward, clasped them, and covered them with kisses.

"Ma'am—Delphinium! You are so beautiful," he stammered.

"Oh, Arthur!" Delphie sighed.

Patricia cleared her throat and said, "Good afternoon, Captain Farell."

The young officer went red in the face and released Delphie's hands. "Beg your pardon—beg you to understand—my feelings for Miss Harmon spring from deep respect—"

As he stammered on, Patricia heard rustling sounds on the other side of the hedge. "Pss-st," an urgent voice whispered. "Hi, there—Pat!"

Freddy was not tall enough to be seen behind the prickly hawthorn bushes, but Patricia recognized his voice. Thinking he had come to tease his sister, she went close to the hedge and whispered, "Go away, Freddy."

"Take a d-damper, Pat! I'm not going anywhere till I talk to you. It is," Freddy insisted, "a m-matter of life and d-death."

Patricia glanced over her shoulder. Delphie and her captain were standing handfast and gazing soulfully into each other's eyes. "I cannot leave these two lovebirds now," she demurred.

"Wiggy's there, ain't she?" Freddy demanded. "I tell you, Pat, I've g-got to talk to you."

He evidently meant what he said. Patricia telegraphed her intentions to Miss Wigge then walked around the hedge to face Freddy. "What is this matter of life and death?" she demanded.

"Lord Longe's come b-back to Riverway," he replied.

Patricia's heart gave an inexplicable leap. As

much irritated by this unwarranted occurrence as with Freddy's dramatics, she said tartly, "I cannot see why this should send you into such a pucker."

"Ain't it just like a female not to let a chap finish?" Freddy wanted to know. "Look, I heard the pater talking to Mama just a few m-moments ago. Charteris means to denounce Lord Longe as the c-coward of Talavera. At the ball, I mean."

Patricia frowned. "But that is nothing new."

"Yes 'tis. Charteris is going to accuse Lord Longe p-publicly. People might ignore rumors about the Duke of Parton's son, but they won't be able to shunt off a thing like this."

Patricia realized the extent of the colonel's cunning. With such people as Lady Were, word would spread quickly throughout the county. And when the Sussex gentry descended on London for the Season, Lord Longshanks's infamy would become the talk of the town. The scurrilous song that the colonel's groom now sang at the White Dragon would become familiar in modish drawing rooms. It would be whistled at Almack's and at White's and all the clubs. Talavera would become an *on-dit* at all the fashionable parties.

Lord Longe would be derided, shunned. Even those who had till now stood his friends would begin to draw away lest mud stick to them.

Once Patricia had wanted Lord Longshanks's disgrace, had wanted it with her whole heart. Now that same heart could not bear the thought of Lord Longe suffering at Charteris's hands. The duke's son was decent and honorable and kind. In fact, Lord Jonathan Longe was a much finer man than the colonel.

"But Charteris is cow-hearted, Freddy," she argued. "Surely he will not risk Lord Longe calling him out."

"He d-don't have to." In his agitation Freddy's stammer worsened. "I heard the p-pater s-say as clear as daylight that if Lord Longe sends his c-cartel, Charteris will toss it into the fire. He'll tell everyone that it's b-beneath his dignity to c-cross swords with the coward of Talavera."

Chapter Ten

In the hush that followed Freddy's announcement, a blackbird began its song. That cheerful sound served to underscore the viciousness of what Patricia had just heard.

"Nothing's going to s-stop the pater from following through with his plans," Freddy was warning. "He's beside the bridge unless Charteris m-marries Delphie, so he's toad-eating the bounder."

Patricia suddenly recalled that she was supposed to be playing chaperon. "We can at least warn Lord Longe," she decided. "He will know what must be done. Seamus will take a note to Riverway as soon as I return to the house."

Somewhat comforted, Freddy went off to write the note, and Patricia retraced her steps. She found Miss Wigge had turned her back to the young couple, who were sitting together on a marble bench ornamented with roses and cupids.

Delphie's golden head rested on Captain Farell's

shoulder, and their hands were clasped together. As Patricia entered the garden, the captain was protesting, "Dash it all, can't help feeling uneasy—not the sort of thing a gentleman can countenance, don't you know."

"Arthur, dearest, it is the *only* way. Will you do it for me?"

Passionately Captain Farell began to kiss Delphie's hands meanwhile begging her to believe that he would be cut into little pieces, boiled in oil, and devoured by wild beasts for her sake.

"But," he added, "*this* goes against the grain."

"It goes against *my* grain to be married to the colonel, Arthur."

About to protest further, Captain Farell saw Patricia. He immediately loosed Delphie's hands and got to his feet exclaiming, "Very well, Delphinium—Miss Harmon, I mean—I will do my duty. Good-bye, ma'am."

Miss Wigge looked up from a rosebush she had been pretending to examine. " 'Farewell is such sweet sorrow,' " she quoted mistily.

"Do not forget what we—do not forget," Delphie urged.

"On my life, I'll remember, don't you know."

The captain bowed with his hand on his heart and strode off. Miss Wigge murmured, " 'So faithful in love and so dauntless in war—' what a pity that all men are not like him."

Patricia threw all that remained of her good sense to the winds. "Delphie," she cried, "you must not marry Colonel Charteris. Refuse and keep on refusing. Your parents cannot drag you to the altar!"

Delphie sighed.

"I will talk to them," Patricia vowed. "Depend

on it, I will convince Aunt Maria that you are too pretty to be wasted away on a mere colonel. What is he but the brother of a viscount, after all? I will tell Aunt that you should marry an earl. Or a—or a *duke*."

"But I have decided to marry Colonel Charteris," Delphie interrupted.

Patricia stared hard at her cousin. "What did you say?"

"If I do not marry Colonel Charteris, the family will be ruined," Delphie replied quite calmly. "I do not want to marry a duke, Patricia. If I cannot have Arthur, I do not care who my husband is. You must not tease me for I have made up my mind."

Delphie had caved in to pressure from her family. Patricia had never felt so dismal as she did at this moment. No doubt it was the only sensible thing to do, and no doubt her aunt and uncle felt that Delphie would be happy as the colonel's lady, but the thought of marriage to Charteris was unspeakable.

Her cousin's decision lay heavy on Patricia's heart later when she took Freddy's note and went to find Seamus. He was in the stable groaning and rubbing his back. "Sure, and don't I have the lumbago again?" he grumbled. "It must have come on me that damp day when I rode to the colonel's with your message, Miss Patricia."

If Seamus was wracked by lumbago, he could not go to Riverway. While she coaxed the old groom to lie down and promised to send a lineament for his back, Patricia rearranged her plans.

None of the servants in the house were trustworthy enough to take a warning to Lord Longe. "They would tell Uncle Hector, and that would never do," she mused. "Freddy must take Argos and go."

Freddy was willing, but fortune was not with him. Mimsby chanced to see him as he was on his way out of the side door and advanced upon him in a threatening way.

"Now what is this, Mr. Harmon?" the burly valet demanded. "You sneezed twice this morning, and Lady Burgess was most emphatic that you remain in your room. If you do not go there at once, sir, I shall be forced to inform her ladyship."

Freddy was so incensed that he choked and began to cough. This set the seal on his doom, for Lady Burgess heard him. Emerging from the morning room, she begged her son to repair immediately to his room in order to submit to a footbath.

Before he was sent into exile, Freddy managed a moment alone with his cousin. "I'm going to strangle Mimsby and throw his body in the river," he vowed bitterly. "I'm s-sorry about this, Pat, but you've got to go to Riverway and warn Lord Longe. There's no other way."

As Freddy said, there was no choice in the matter; but as she mounted Argos, Patricia realized the irony of what she was about to do. She who had sworn to ruin Lord Longe was now trying to help him. "Seamus would say that curses always came home to roost," Patricia muttered to herself. "Oh, hell and the devil, what a coil this is."

It was late afternoon when she set out. Sunlight filtered like gold dust on the green downs, picked out dandelions and cowslips and daisies with yellow hearts. A herd of white-faced sheep looked curiously up at her from a rolling pasture, and a lacy butterfly danced on Argos's pommel.

Patricia's mind was not on the beauty of the scenery. As she took the easterly fork in the road, her skittish thoughts flew in many directions. She recalled Jack's wounds and his pain. She remembered how furious she had been when she first heard the story of Talavera. Then she thought of the day she had met Lord Longe and the way he had kissed her and held her close to his strong, lean body.

Lost in her memories, she neared Riverway Place. The sun was poised just over the horizon, and each window of the fine old house was blazing with sunset. Sunset colors played on the Leads River, and an evening breeze brought the scent of water and earth, reminding Patricia of the day of the storm.

"I only want what you can give with your whole heart," Lord Longe had said that day. She had not then understood what he had meant, but now—

Patricia's heart had begun to beat erratically, and she couldn't seem to catch her breath. She couldn't even think too clearly. Out of all her tangled emotions, one thought surfaced, and this was that she didn't want to face Lord Longe. If the whole truth be told, she did not *dare*.

She was preparing to turn Argos and ride back to Burgess Hall when a familiar voice exclaimed, "I am certain of it now."

Lord Longe was standing not ten yards away. He was leaning against a willow tree that grew by the river edge and talking to a man that Patricia did not recognize. This gentleman was tall and, in spite of the unseasonably warm March evening, was bundled into a heavy cape.

Lord Longe was holding a few pebbles which he tossed at intervals into the water. His face was in the shadow, but Patricia could somehow sense his tension as he said, "No question about it. It was cowardice—damnable, inexcusable cowardice."

The unknown gentleman said something Patricia couldn't catch.

"You're right," Lord Longe agreed. "This is proof positive. You know, I never thought that it would come to this. The Board of Inquiry's findings were so conclusive." Suddenly he burst out, "God knows that I can't forget those poor fellows at Talavera."

Patricia sat her horse and listened to each damning word. But instead of hating Lord Longe, her heart was torn for his pain. No use to try and hide from the truth any longer, Patricia thought. In spite of everything she knew about him, she had fallen in love with Lord Longshanks.

Why and how this had happened, she didn't know. She did know that she had struggled against her emotions without avail. Even when she had tried to hate him, he had remained in her mind—and in her heart.

Lord Longe was decent and kind. How he must have suffered for his one mistake at Talavera. But when he had tried to explain to her, she had not even tried to listen. Patricia's eyes filled with tears as she recalled how self-righteous she had been.

As if he sympathized with his mistress's unhappiness, Argos whinnied softly, and the two men by the water's edge turned their heads. "Good Lord," Lord Longe exclaimed, "it's Miss Surrey."

He came forward at once exclaiming, "This is an unexpected pleasure. I've been meaning to come to—why are you crying?"

Patricia noted that the muffled stranger was walking painfully toward Riverway House. She gave a determined sniff and said, "I am not crying. There is—there is something in my eye."

"Let me help you down." She did not want to dismount, but when he held out his arms, she couldn't help leaning down and sliding into them. He held her close against his lean, hard length for a moment, and then with obvious reluctance loosed her.

"Let me see your eye," he said. Patricia gave a strangled hiccup. "You *are* crying. Why, my dearest love?"

She didn't have any defense against the tenderness in his voice. "Oh, Jonathan," Patricia gulped, "it is too horrible for words."

Lord Longe did not bother to ask what was so horrible. He had called her his love. Instead of rebuking him, she was looking up at him with tear-dazzled eyes. Nothing on heaven or earth could prevent him from kissing her now.

She lifted her lips for his kiss, and for a moment the whole world seemed to stand still. It was as if the setting sun had suddenly halted in its descent so that it could enfold them in golden light.

"I love you, Patricia," Lord Longe said.

She had the feeling that in his arms nothing evil or sad could ever touch her again. Tremulously Patricia smiled up at the man she had sworn to hate all her life.

"I love you, too," she sighed.

Lord Longe wasn't sure whether he was dreaming, but he didn't think so. The slender form in his arms felt very real. Her voice, which had just declared her love for him, sounded real as well. Just to make sure, he drew her close and felt the beat of her heart against his chest.

"I've wanted to hold you like this." Fervently he kissed the dimple in her chin. "I've dreamed of kissing you here. And here. I want to devote my whole life kissing you, Patricia."

Suddenly she remembered why she had come to Riverway. "Jonathan," she began, "I must warn you—"

"Later," he said, and lowered his lips to hers.

Lack of oxygen finally drove them apart, and they leaned against each other, dazed, exhausted, and blissful. At last Patricia stirred, "Jonathan?" she murmured.

"Yes, my love."

"Colonel Charteris is going to ruin you."

He smiled. "I know that."

She leaned away from him and looked searchingly into his face. "Do you also know that he is going to denounce you publicly in front of my aunt's and uncle's guests?"

So that was it, Lord Longe thought. Percival Yancey had told him that Charteris was drinking heavily as though to give himself Dutch courage.

"I was sure that he'd show his hand," Lord Longe mused, "but I didn't know when or where. Now, thanks to you, I do."

He bent a suddenly searching look on her. "Patricia, why are you warning me? Remember that once you swore never to forgive me."

"I meant what I said—then."

"And now?"

"Now I know that you are honorable and courageous." Conviction filled Patricia's voice as she continued, "I do not know what really happened at Talavera, Jonathan, for I was not there. I do not know the circumstances that made you act as you did. What I do know is that it is wrong for me—for anyone—to judge you."

"Then you forgive me for causing your brother's wounds?"

She hesitated, and Lord Longe could almost read her thoughts. She was thinking of Jack, wounded and weak. Every preconceived hatred she had had for Lord Longshanks was now warring against the love that had grown in spite of her.

"Patricia," he said, "look at me."

Troubled, she met his eyes. The setting sun had turned his dark hair to a deep bronze, and his eyes were almost silver. She had never seen him look so stern.

"Do you believe in me?" he demanded.

Suddenly something hard and tight seemed to loosen inside Patricia, and she spoke from her heart. "Yes," she cried, "yes, Jonathan. I believe in you."

Lord Longe hadn't known he was holding his breath. Now he let it go in one deep, heartfelt sigh.

"Then we will win through. Don't worry about Charteris, my love. I'll deal with him."

For a moment Patricia was convinced by the exultant note in his voice. Then, she remembered something else that Freddy had said.

"Jonathan, if you send him your cartel, Charteris will say that it is beneath him to meet a coward. How can you fight a man like that?"

He bent and kissed her so that she would not see the suddenly grim expression in his eyes. "With the truth," he said.

"Wiggy, how do I look?"

"Like a veritable flower, Miss Delphinium. 'There

is a garden in her face, Where roses and white lilies grow,'—as Campion says."

Delphie pirouetted in front of her mirror. "This is a very important night for me. It marks the end of my girlhood, Wiggy."

She paused as her mother came sweeping into the room. "Well, Mama?" she asked, brightly. "Do I look fine enough for my betrothal?"

"Delphinium, I always knew that you would be a good, sensible girl."

Lady Burgess had tears in her eyes as she glided forward to kiss her daughter's cheek. Patricia, standing in the hallway, saw an odd look flit across her cousin's face.

"Depend upon it, my dear," Lady Burgess said, "you will not be sorry about this match."

"Oh, no, Mama."

"People in our circles do not marry for *love*." Lady Burgess pronounced the word disdainfully. "It is much better to be guided by reason than be a slave to vulgar emotions." She patted Delphie's cheek with a gloved hand. "Collect that you will have all manner of luxury and servants and a house in London during the Season. And, since the Viscount Teglare is an unmarried man, you will no doubt be a viscountess one day."

"No doubt, Mama."

Since she had announced to her parents that she would marry Colonel Charteris, Delphie had made an abrupt volte-face. She was now as demure and as tractable as her mother could wish. Patricia didn't understand why this change made her feel so uneasy. She knew that she should be glad that Delphie had a bedrock of hard sense and was making the best of things.

"Miss Delphinium looks like Aurora tonight," Miss Wigge enthused.

The governess's eyes were snapping excitedly, and her lips were pursed tight as though holding back some delicious secret. " 'She walks in beauty like the night," she rhapsodized, "Of cloudless climes and starry skies—' "

"Wiggy," Delphie interposed firmly, "hush."

Miss Wigge stopped in midquote and looked guilty. "I know what you would say, my love," she cried. "You are right. I should not repeat what such a man as Lord Byron writes. He is a sad rake, and his works are unfit for chaste ears. Besides which, Aurora is the goddess of dawn and not night at all. The metaphors are mixed since it is night now and not morning."

Lady Burgess blinked several times before giving this up. "Will you walk down with Delphinium, my dear?" she asked her niece. "I am going now to make sure that all is ready for our guests and my dear, good daughter."

As she left the room, Patricia once more saw that strange expression pass across Delphie's face.

"Delphie," she said, "are you *sure* that this is what you want to do?"

Instantly Delphie's expression returned to normal. She shrugged prettily and said, "Talking and tears will not mend fences. If I do not marry a man with money, the family will be penniless. I do not want to be impoverished, so my duty is plain."

Miss Wigge made an odd sound that could have been either a sob or a chuckle, and Patricia realized that everyone's nerves were tightly strained.

"I will love Arthur forever," Delphie continued tragically, "but as Mama says, persons of our class do not marry for love. I must make the most advantageous match possible." She whisked out a diminutive bit of lace and wiped a tear from the corner of her eye. "I will conceal my broken heart from the world."

Now, that sounded, more like Delphie. Patricia didn't want to think of what might happen when her cousin finally realized that she was not playing a part in a romantic play.

In the meantime Delphie looked radiant. Her new dress of cream-colored satin had been the pride of its Bond Street creator. Satin ribbons and small roses had been braided into her hair, which was dressed in the Greek style. There were satin slippers on her feet, and the fan she carried was made of ivory and white ostrich feathers.

The thought flashed through Patricia's mind that Delphie looked more like a happy bride than someone who was secretly nursing a broken heart.

"Dear Patricia, you are not to worry about me. You must come downstairs and enjoy the ball." Delphie paused and then dimpled to add, "I am persuaded that it will be an exciting evening."

In more ways than one, Patricia thought. Since her ride to Riverway, she had been torn between joy and fear for Lord Longe. He had not told her what he planned to do, but her instinct told her that he would come to the ball tonight and force the colonel to face him.

Though she hadn't told even Freddy her suspicion, Patricia had dressed for action. In case she needed to move quickly for whatever reason, her dress of blue gossamer satin decorated with roses and seed pearls was cut fashionably short. Her curls had been caught simply to one side in the Roman style and were accented by a single rose. On her feet Patricia wore becoming but sensible blue slippers.

"You look very pretty, Patricia," Delphie was saying. "One would think that you had dressed to impress a particular gentleman. Who, I wonder?"

She spread open her fan and smiled roguishly at her cousin, who rather hastily said that she was ready to go down. "Are you coming also, Miss Wigge?"

The governess shook her head. "Though Lady Burgess was gracious enough to invite me," she fluttered, "I hope that I know my place. Enjoy yourself, dear Miss Delphinium and Miss Surrey, and remember the words of Herbert, who said, 'He that lives in hope danceth without musick.' "

Her quotations pursued them down the stairs of a transformed house, which had been scrubbed and refurbished and polished to an inch of its life. Servants had erected a canopy of gold cloth over the front door and rolled out a length of red carpet into the courtyard so that guests would not need to soil their shoes after alighting from their carriages. This carpet continued into the house and up the stairs to the first floor and the great hall, where the dancing was to take place.

An orchestra was tuning up on the first floor, and Charms was directing servants to set up trays of wines and tidbits with which to tempt the guests' appetite in advance of the formal dinner.

None of the guests had yet arrived, and the great hall, guarded by no liveried footmen, was empty. Delphie peeped into this usually cavernous and gloomy chamber and exclaimed, "As Freddy would say, Mama has pulled out all the stops."

Certainly no expense had been spared for the Burgess's ball. Tonight the great hall was a place of pleasure. Garlands of early spring flowers, hot-house roses, and ivy were hung everywhere, and new curtains of crimson and gold gave the windows a regal look. Mirrors had been polished, portraits and statuary dusted, and hundreds of scented candles that blazed in the chandeliers. Nor had the smaller details been overlooked: new crimson cushions graced mahogany chairs and aromatic wood burned in the huge fireplace.

Freddy was warming his hands before this fire, very conscious of his new blue coat with the padded shoulders, and his neck cloth, which he had attempted, in spite of Mimsby's objections, to tie in the waterfall style.

"Dashed rum b-business," he exclaimed when he saw his sister and cousin. "Can't think why you're looking s-so happy, Delphie."

"Would it help to be Friday-faced?"

Swaying gracefully, Delphie walked away and arranged herself artistically in a chair. Freddy shook his head. "Been raising a peal about being b-buckled to Charteris, and now look at her." He lowered his voice. "What's Lord Longe going to do, Pat, can you think?"

She shook her head. "He only said that he would deal with the colonel. How, I do not know."

Freddy said bluntly, "He b-better do something before Charteris opens his mouth. Once the word's out, some mud's bound to stick."

Lord Burgess now trotted in, stared hard at his son, and requested him in pained accents to go upstairs and change his cravat.

"It looks like something the cat didn't want," he

177

declared. "What's that ass Mimsby thinking of, letting you out looking like that?" Then, as Freddy dejectedly left the room, he added, "Where's Charteris, hey? The man's late."

Patricia walked away without comment, and Lord Burgess muttered a round oath to himself. He was feeling uneasy. The ball had seemed to be a good thing at the onset, but the expense was staggering, and there was also this denunciation of Lord Longe.

Charteris insisted upon it, but Maria had been all a-twitter and for once Lord Burgess did not blame his wife. It did not seem good *ton* to accuse a duke's son of cowardice publicly. Of course it was all Longe's fault for coming to Sussex in the first place, but even so—

Lord Burgess's thoughts groaned to a stop as his first guest was announced. Tonight Lady Were resembled a malicious thistle in her purple gown and matching turban. She aimed several barbed comments at her host then captured Patricia and commenced a running commentary derogatory to each guest that arrived.

Patricia did not hear half of what was said. She was busy watching the door through which walked every person of consequence in the county. Lord and Lady Yancey and their sons were there. The Countess Ballingford was there. So were the Viscount Porter, and Major Lord Jermyn Armstead, and many others whose names were listed among the Ten Thousand. Some who had already gone to London had even returned to Sussex for the ball. The thought that Lord Longe could be humiliated before all these people made Patricia feel queasy.

Sometime after eight o'clock, a familiar, booming voice arose from the ground floor anteroom. Lord

Burgess and his lady hastened to greet their guest of honor and escort him to the great hall. When they returned, Patricia noted that though there was a suspicious redness to the colonel's nose, he did not seem to be actually drunk.

"Delphinium has been waiting anxiously for your arrival, Colonel," Lady Burgess fluttered.

Patricia glanced at her cousin, who was flirting with some young men who had grouped themselves around her. She did not lose her composure when her suitor marched to her side and trumpeted that she was even more beautiful than ever.

How *could* she remain so calm? Patricia wondered as Delphie returned the colonel's greetings cheerfully. Even the news that Captain Farell had taken to his bed with an undisclosed ailment did not make her change countenance.

"Miss Surrey, your most obedient."

Mr. Yancey had strolled up to Patricia and was making an elegant bow. Attired in fashionably tight pantaloons, black waistcoat embroidered with flowers, and an exquisitely tied cravat, he looked bored but amiable.

Mr. Yancey was Lord Longe's friend. Perhaps *he* knew what his lordship's plans could be. While she murmured polite inconsequentials, Patricia wondered how she could phrase a question.

"I had heard that Lord Longe was back from Scotland," she began.

"Oh, was he in Scotland?" Mr. Yancey polished his quizzing glass on his sleeve and held it to his eye. "Nincompoop, ain't he? I mean Charteris, of course."

"No," Patricia said. "That is to say, yes, he is a nincompoop, but he is also dangerous."

Mr. Yancey turned his round, shrewd countenance toward her. "You're worried about Jonathan, ma'am," he said. "No need, give you m'word. He can take care of himself."

Patricia was not so sure. "He is the son of a duke," she murmured. "He has no idea what will happen if people believe he is a—if people believe the colonel."

She looked about her at the dazzling throng of guests who had all unknowingly gathered to witness Lord Longe's public humiliation. Lady Were wasn't the only one who would spread gossip and slander. Those young ladies who were flirting with their admirers would turn up their pert noses at Lord Longe. Their mamas would not receive him. Their papas and brothers would blackball him from their clubs.

Suddenly the room seemed full not of Sussex aristocracy, but of birds of prey. Patricia felt sickened. Excusing herself, she left the great hall and searched the ground floor anteroom hopefully, but as yet there was no sign of a tall man with gray eyes. The sick feeling in Patricia grew worse.

Just then she heard the rattle of wheels out in the courtyard. Hastily crossing the hall, Patricia looked out of a many-paned window. She could see the many carriages, curricles, phaetons, and barouches standing in the drizzle outside, but there was no sign of Lord Longe's curricle. "Perhaps," Patricia murmured, "he is not going to come."

"I say—Pat!"

A grim-faced Freddy was at her elbow. "Charteris is getting r-ready to make his little speech," he said.

"Oh, he cannot," Patricia cried despairingly. "Not yet."

But now they could hear Lord Burgess introducing his guest. "C-come on, Pat," Freddy urged. "Lord Longe needs his friends to be there."

Patricia gave the dark courtyard another desperate glance before following Freddy back to the great hall. Here her uncle was praising his guest of honor.

"My new neighbor—yours, too. Hey? He's a newcomer, a young man who's made his mark. A gallant soldier and a gentleman who has the ear of the Viscount Wellington. Soon to be connected to my family—but more of that later. Now Colonel Waldo Charteris will say a few words to you."

Lord Burgess made way for the colonel, who clasped his hands behind his back, rocked on his heels, and glanced complacently about him.

"My lords and ladies," he began. "No, let me call you friends. I am never too grand, I hope, to stand on ceremony."

"P-pompous ass," Freddy growled.

"I'm honored to be here among you. However, there's one man among us that I cannot consider either my friend or my neighbor."

Patricia gripped Freddy's arm tightly. "Perhaps you know that I have served my country honorably on the Peninsula," the colonel went on. "It was during the battle of Talavera, in fact, that I met Lord Longe."

A distinguished, gray-haired gentleman—Lord Yancey—interrupted at this point. "I don't see Jonathan Longe anywhere," he challenged. "Do you intend to malign him behind his back?"

Young Mr. Yancey exclaimed, "Here, here!" and

several other guests nodded their heads. Seeing this, Colonel Charteris changed his strategy.

His square face lengthened into an expression of feigned sorrow. His protuberant eyes widened with the effort of conveying his sincerity.

"I beg you to believe I have no personal malice against Lord Longe. It is a sense of duty that compels me to tell you all that I saw with my own eyes. Sir Arthur Wellesley—Viscount Wellington, I mean—once said, 'Charteris, you must do your duty,' and no matter how painful I must follow his command. Lord Longe has the blood of the Nineteenth Foot Guard on his hands."

Patricia could almost see a ripple of uneasiness undulate through the room. Lady Were craned her neck forward as Lord Yancey snapped, "I've heard these allegations before, Charteris. I told you I don't believe a word of it. I only came tonight to make sure Jonathan got a fair hearing."

"My lord, I wish that I had not seen what I saw. You see, I was in command of an artillery division at Talavera. My own aide, Captain Philip Oranger, was killed in the action. A grievous loss." The colonel placed his hand on his heart as he added, "Sir Arthur was good enough to comfort me. 'Charteris,' he said, 'you have sustained the loss of a friend.'"

The guests murmured amongst themselves. Lord Burgess had been right when he said that many of the Sussex aristocracy had lost someone in the war. The Countess Bellingford had lost a cousin, and the Viscount Porter's brother had been grievously wounded. If Jonathan didn't arrive soon, Patricia thought, it might be too late.

Colonel Charteris was saying, "My friends, I regret to say that with my own eyes I saw Lord Long-shanks turn tail and run in the face of enemy fire."

"Liar!"

Patricia's impassioned voice cut through the colonel's speech. "You are lying," she repeated. "How could you possibly have seen Lord Longe? Your artillery was positioned miles away from the Nineteenth Foot Guard."

The colonel's smile was patronizing. "I suppose that you are an expert in military strategy, Miss Surrey?"

Hands clenched, Freddy sprang forward. "If you don't s-speak to my cousin civilly," he threatened, "I'll s-serve you some home brewed."

Lord Burgess gave a yelp of horror. He trundled across the room, caught his son by the collar, and shook him. Lady Burgess looked ready to faint. Lord Yancey and his wife began to protest that they had known Lord Longe since childhood and did not believe a word of Colonel Charteris's story while at the same time half a dozen other voices exclaimed that it was just as they'd thought—there'd always been something smoky about Longe.

Above their combined voices rose Lady Were's silky tones. "I am persuaded the colonel speaks truth," she declared. "There has always been an instability in Parton's family. Make no mistake, Jonathan Longe is a loose fish."

"If what you say is true, he's a despicable coward," an elderly gentleman cried. "My son was killed at Talavera."

Patricia advanced to the center of the room. "This is England," she cried. "How can you condemn a man without a hearing? You Lady Were, entertained Lord Longe in your home. How could you have done so if you felt that he was 'unstable'? Lord Vrennon, you have hunted with him, for I have heard you remark on his prowess as a horseman. You, Countess, told my aunt that he was a most delightful man. Hypocrites, the lot of you!"

"Patricia," moaned Lady Burgess.

Patricia clenched her hands. "You should be ashamed of yourselves," she cried.

Before she could continue, Charms came to the portals of the great hall. In a choked voice he announced, "Lord Longe."

Patricia whipped about to see the duke's son standing in the doorway of the great hall. He was dressed in a long-tailed coat of dark gray superfine and knee-breeches of the same hue. His cambric shirt, cut in the Brummell fashion, was elegance itself as was his simply tied black cravat. His hair gleamed like the glossy wing of a raven as he bowed to the assembly.

"I am sorry that I am late," he said.

His smile embraced Patricia for a moment, and her heart overflowed with relief and pride and love. He had come after all. Then the inevitable question surfaced. What could he do to still the emotions that were already seething in the room?

As she anxiously searched his face, she realized for the first time that a gentleman stood behind Lord Longe. It was the same tall man whom she had seen at Riverway. Though his face was half hidden by a riding cloak, Patricia noted that he was thin and pale and that his dark eyes were fixed on Colonel Charteris.

"This gentleman is the reason for my being late," Lord Longe was explaining. "I beg your pardon, Burgess. You said something?"

Looking to be on the point of an apoplexy, the baronet snapped, "You're not welcome here, Longe, and so I tell you."

"Shame," Lady Were fluted. "The coward of Talavera."

A rakish-looking young man began to whistle the tune to that familiar ditty, but Mr. Yancey strolled over to him and whispered something that caused instant silence. Gray-headed Lord Yancey exclaimed sternly, "I'm glad you are here, Jonathan. Now, Charteris can continue."

Angrily the colonel began, "The man wasn't invited. He should—"

Then he broke off, staring as the tall man who had accompanied Lord Longe dropped the folds of his cloak from around his face.

"Colonel Charteris," he said, "do you believe in ghosts?"

Chapter Eleven

"Allow me to present myself," the pale gentleman said. "I am Captain Philip Oranger, late aide to Colonel Charteris."

Lord Burgess goggled. "Hey?" he stammered, "did—did you say, *late* aide?"

A convulsive shudder shook the colonel. "My God, Philip, I thought you were dead!"

He strode forward, but Captain Oranger ignored the colonel's outstretched hand. "I crave your pardon," he said, "but I am still very weak. May I have a chair?"

Lord Longe pushed a wing-backed chair forward. As Captain Oranger sank into it, Lord Burgess sputtered, "I don't know what's going on, but it all sounds damned smoky. Look here, young man, I want an explanation."

Captain Oranger's smile was a grimace of pain. Recognizing his sickroom pallor and the sunken, fever-bright eyes, Patricia bit her lip. This man had been ill almost to death and was still much too weak for any excitement.

She looked uncertainly at Lord Longe, who shook his head slightly, enjoining silence. "Are you feeling well enough to continue, Captain Oranger?" he asked.

"It is what I have come for."

"But, my dear boy, this is marvelous," the colonel was trumpeting. "I was convinced you had been killed."

Again he attempted to shake hands, and once more his former aide ignored the gesture. Colonel Charteris flushed and dropped his hand to his side.

"Why have you come here?" he asked abruptly.

Ignoring his former chief, Captain Oranger said, "Lord Burgess, I ask your indulgence. I had heard that Colonel Charteris was going to entertain you with a battlefield story tonight. I have come to tell you my own version of what happened at Talavera."

The assembled guests murmured uneasily. The baronet scowled, but before he could protest, Mr. Yancey drawled, "Bedad, this is becoming interesting. Let's hear it, Captain."

"We had driven the French out of Portugal in May of that year," the captain commenced. "The French commander, Marshal Victor, withdrew to Madrid. In July we met the French at Talavera, on the banks of the Tagus, in a battle that lasted two days."

Captain Oranger's voice faltered, and Patricia signaled a wide-eyed servant to take him some water.

After refreshing himself the captain continued, "The French gun batteries were merciless. The cannon and musket fire was intense. On the English side, Colonel Charteris directed our artillery."

The colonel quickly added, "Our cannonade held those frogs back. I was proud of my men, many of whom sacrificed their lives while doing their duty." He paused and then added modestly, "Naturally I was there with the brave fellows."

"That is not how I remember it," Captain Oranger interposed. "On the morning of the second day, you were lying drunk in your tent."

In the uproar that followed, the colonel's protests were drowned out. "Drunk? did he say, 'drunk'?" Lady Were cried, while Lord Yancey declared that the truth was finally coming out.

Lord Longe's stern voice cut through the noise. "Captain Oranger has not yet finished. I must ask you to give him a full hearing."

The guests hushed at once except for Lady Were, who was still repeating the word, 'drunk.' "This is an outrage," the colonel sputtered. "Oranger's wounds have affected his wits. I did not come here to be insulted by a bedlamite."

"I do not think it possible to insult you, Charteris," his former aide retorted.

Lord Burgess belatedly dismissed the servants. It was an empty gesture. Everyone knew that they would soon have their ears pressed to the door.

As soon as the room was quiet again, Captain Oranger explained that as Charteris's aide, he had carried the colonel's orders to the gun batteries.

"On that second morning at Talavera, I entered the colonel's quarters to receive his orders. These concerned the coordinates for our northern gun battery. The colonel was snoring in a drunken stupor and cursed me when I woke him."

Colonel Charteris began to speak but was silenced by the other guests. "Let the captain have his say," the Earl of Bellingford ordered.

"The colonel told me that his orders were lying on his cot and ordered me to take them to the gunners. Accordingly I took this piece of paper and was carrying them to the gun batteries when my horse was shot from under me. Soon afterward a French ball pierced my throat."

Oranger drew down the collar of his cloak and disclosed an ugly, jagged scar. "I staunched the wound as best as I could and continued on foot. As I handed the colonel's coordinates to our gunners, I was shot in the chest. This time, I fainted."

He had been left for dead—would have died except for a Spanish peasant who was looting the bodies of the slain. The man had found a flutter of pulse and instead of killing the wounded Englishman took him home and cared for him.

"I was very near to death," Captain Oranger told his now spellbound audience, "but I had to live." Suddenly he rose from his chair and pointed directly at the colonel. "I needed to accuse Colonel Waldo Charteris of being so drunk that he gave me the coordinates *of the preceding day*. Because of his mistake, the Nineteenth Foot Guard was fired upon by *English* cannons!"

"He's lying!"

With a roar Colonel Charteris sprang upon his former aide. Lord Longe blocked his way.

"I think not," he said.

Catching the colonel's arm, Lord Longe twisted it behind his back. The colonel bellowed with pain. "Damn you to hell," he shouted. "Let me go!"

Lord Longe pushed the colonel backward. Charteris staggered across the room, fetched up against a chair, and sank into it. "Burgess," he shouted, "how can you allow these madmen to enact a Cheltenham Tragedy in your house?"

Thus appealed to, the baronet found his voice. "You've made some serious accusations, Oranger. Hey? What proof do you have that what you're telling us is true? You were wounded, man. You could have been mistaken."

"That's right," the colonel cried desperately. "You were mistaken, Philip. Longe's headlong retreat brought his troops into the line of our cannonade. That was it, wasn't it?"

Captain Oranger replied, "Just before I lost consciousness, I saw our cannons fire the first volley. The ball fell directly into the position held by the Nineteenth Foot Guard."

Lord Burgess saw that most of his guests were eyeing Colonel Charteris with horror. Suddenly he realized that he was standing on the edge of a precipice.

The dream of a son-in-law who would be rich enough to pay all his debts and restore him to prosperity was rapidly vanishing. Instead, he saw himself as others would see him: a gull-catcher, a fool, a dupe. Like a drowning man, he clung to the one hope he had left.

"I want proof," he insisted. "Hey? It's your word against the colonel's."

It was Lord Longe who replied, "You shall have your proof."

He strode to the closed door and swung it open. An elderly man in the uniform of an artilleryman now walked into the room.

"Mr. Owens," Patricia exclaimed.

As Owens saluted, the colonel sneered, "That's the tramp I thrashed the other day. Is *he* your precious proof?"

Owens abandoned his military posture. "You mean you *tried* ter thrash me, you bully," he said wrathfully. "The guv'nor 'ere wouldn't stand fer it, though."

"Artilleryman," Lord Longe commanded, "give your evidence."

Owens snapped back to attention. "Sir! I was on the north gun battery during the Battle o' Talavera. I was there when we got those coordinates Captain Oranger speaks o'. We followed horders and fired on hour own boys."

Lord Burgess protested, "Surely you could *see* your mistake?"

Owens snorted. "It's plain you wasn't never in a fight, sir. The smoke from the cannon and the muskets was so thick, we couldn't see nofink. And there was cannonballs and shells flying hover'ead, and there was the screams o' the dying, and the road were clogged with wounded and baggage trains—Lord, it was a mercy we knew hour own names. Firing blind, we was, trusting in hour horders from Colonel Charteris."

"So he *did* order you to fire on the Nineteenth Foot Guard," Lord Yancey exclaimed.

"As sure as I'm standing 'ere, sir, 'e did. Them poor buggers of the Nineteenth 'ad it coming and going. They was in battle square formation when we fired on them. They 'eld, even though they was being blowed to 'ell, but then the French coo-raiseers—them being Boney's cavalry—charged them. I 'eard that's when their horficer got 'is senses, like, and got 'is men the 'ell out of it."

191

"If you knew so much," Lord Burgess sneered, "why didn't you speak up before this?"

"Our horficers was killed in the battle, and hour sergeant, too. Most o' the lads on the guns was killed or wounded bad like I was." Owens tapped his leg significantly before adding, "While I was in the bleeding 'orspital, I 'eard that Colonel Charteris' 'ad spread rumors that the Nineteenth Foot Guard 'ad been cut down acourse Lord Longe had run in the face of Frenchy fire. Colonel Charteris is an horficer and a toff and rich ter boot. 'Oo'd take my word over 'is?"

"No one," the colonel snarled. "No one would believe you."

But Lord Yancey shook his head. "I for one believe Owens. You slandered Jonathan Longe, Charteris, because you needed to cover your own horrible blunder."

Hisses of "Shame!" now echoed throughout the great hall, and Colonel Charteris turned the color of farm cheese. "I've heard enough," he grated. "I'm leaving."

He got to his feet, but Lord Longe blocked the way. "Not quite yet," he said. "There's more to be said."

With a bellow, Colonel Charteris rushed at the duke's son. There was a cracking sound, and the colonel yelled, staggered back, and fell to his knees. Blood was flowing from his nose.

"A very whisty c-castor," Freddy approved.

Philip Oranger smiled. "I have wanted to do that all these months, but I can't begrudge you, Lord Longe. I know how Colonel Charteris tried to blacken your name both on the Continent and here in Sussex."

"Shame!" The word was said louder this time, and the guests made haste to assure each other that *they* had never believed the scandalous rumors about Lord Longe.

Charteris had staggered to his feet and was holding a handkerchief to his nose. "Burgess," he pleaded, "these men are lying. Surely you can't believe them."

Lord Burgess turned his back.

"Dastard," Lady Were said in her lovely voice, "to cover your own incompetence by accusing an innocent man."

"Should be horsewhipped, don't you know." Mr. Yancey began to stroll forward as he added. "Bedad, I think I'll do it meself."

Desperately the colonel turned to his hostess. "Surely *you* cannot believe these lies?"

Lady Burgess, who had been on the point of swooning this past half hour, now spoke in a strangled voice. "You have abused the hospitality of this house. You have lied to all your friends. I pray you sir, go—immediately."

The colonel's shoulders slumped in defeat. His eyes turned glassy. Heedless of the blood that was still flowing from his nose, he staggered out of the great hall. Even the footmen, standing at attention outside the door, seemed to shrink from touching him.

Lord Burgess's guests now surged forward to surround Lord Longe. The gentlemen shook his hand, clapped him on the back, and protested their friendship and esteem. The ladies vied with one another to vilify Colonel Charteris.

Though in a turmoil herself at what she had just seen and heard, Patricia was quick to note Captain

Oranger's pallor. Going to his side, she bent over him. "You are ill," she exclaimed.

The captain managed a white-lipped smile. "I have never felt better in my life," he assured her.

Just then Lord Longe turned his head to look for Patricia. Seeing Captain Oranger sink back into his chair and close his eyes, he strode across the room. "I was afraid it would be too much for him," he said worriedly, "but he insisted on having his moment. How is he?"

"He is exhausted and must lie down at once," Patricia replied. "Aunt Maria, may I take Captain Oranger to another room?"

"Of course—yes, do as you see fit." Lady Burgess looked ready to cry, and Patricia felt sorry for her aunt. The ball that had held such promise had become a nightmare. Then another thought came. The colonel's disgrace meant that Delphie wouldn't have to marry him!

Patricia looked around the great hall but could not see her cousin anywhere. No doubt Delphie had run upstairs to inform Miss Wigge of her deliverance. Meanwhile there was Captain Oranger to deal with.

"We will take him across the hall," she decided. "It will be quiet in the yellow saloon. Lord Longe, if you will take one arm and Freddy the other?"

Protesting and apologizing that he did not want to be a bother, the sick man was transported across the hall and laid down on a lacquered daybed in the yellow saloon. While Patricia sent servants scurrying for a shawl and pillows, Lord Longe poured a measure of brandy into a glass and held it to Captain Oranger's lips.

"Drink it down and don't talk," he commanded. "It is over. You have done what you came to do."

As the sick man obediently drained the fiery liquid, Freddy crowed, "So Charteris was to blame for what happened at Talavera. I don't blame you for planting him that facer, sir! But why did he st-start telling lies about you the minute he clapped eyes on you?"

"He was afraid I had come to expose him, perhaps." Oddly enough, now that it was over Lord Longe didn't bear Charteris any ill will. In fact, he felt as lighthearted as a boy.

"It was sheer luck that I befriended Owens," he said. "The old fellow told me he'd come to Sussex after a visit from Captain Oranger's servant. That's how I came to know the captain was alive and in Scotland."

"I was making my own inquiries," the sick man explained. "I needed to find one of the gunners to corroborate my story. I sent a trusted servant to find a survivor among the gunners who had manned the northern cannons. He ran Owens down in London, but instead of telling me that Charteris was in Sussex, Owens went looking for him. I suspect that he meant to blackmail Charteris."

Patricia interrupted by saying firmly that the captain needed to rest.

"Freddy, will you see to it that no one disturbs us?" she asked. "I will sit with the captain for a while."

Freddy went off willingly, and Lord Longe retreated to the French windows and stood looking out over the dark, rain-misted gardens. As soon as the captain had fallen into an exhausted doze, Patricia joined him there.

"All this time you knew the truth about Talavera," she accused.

He shook his head. "No. I *suspected* that the cannon that ripped us to pieces wasn't French, but the Board of Inquiry dismissed my suggestion that we'd been fired on by our own guns. On the word of a gentleman, I had no idea that Charteris was responsible until I spoke with Captain Oranger."

And she had believed the colonel's lies. "Can you forgive me?" Patricia wondered.

"Not unless you marry me."

Patricia felt as if everything in her heart was shifting, falling gently into its rightful place. She smiled up at Lord Longe and whispered, "Of course I will marry you. I love you with all my heart."

But instead of taking her into his arms, he searched her upturned face. "You're sure about this? There's no turning back, my love."

"Why should I want to turn back?" Patricia wondered.

Her mouth was warm and sweet. Lord Longe wanted to kiss that mouth and keep on kissing it, but there was still something that needed to be said.

"Not everyone will be convinced that Charteris was to blame at Talavera, my love. There may be talk—"

"There has been too much talking already." Patricia put her arms around his lordship's neck and added saucily, "Well, my lord?"

He crushed her to him. Their lips met in a kiss that suffocated all conscious thought. Lord Longe and Patricia stood holding each other and swaying to a music that only they could hear. Only a need to breathe drove them apart.

"My sweet love," his lordship murmured, "My darling—"

"My God!"

Lord Burgess's gasp startled the lovers and awakened the sleeping man on the daybed. Patricia would have pulled away from Lord Longe, but he would not let her escape.

"Haven't you ever heard of knocking on a closed door, Burgess?" he asked.

"Hey? Why should I knock on a door in my own house? And never mind that," Lord Burgess added indignantly, "what were you doing kissing my niece?"

Lord Longe's arms tightened about Patricia. "Miss Surrey," he announced, "has consented to marry me."

Captain Oranger struggled to a sitting position. "I wish you both very happy," he was beginning, when Lord Burgess interrupted.

"Oh, no you don't. Hey? She's my niece and under my protection. I'm not going to allow her to marry a loose screw like you."

"Uncle Hector!" Patricia protested.

"You be quiet, miss. Kissing this loose fish and carrying on under my roof like you was a barmaid at an inn."

"Do you carry on with barmaids?" Lord Longe clicked his tongue reprovingly. "I'm surprised at you, Burgess. I thought you to be a respectable family man."

"What're you talking about? I nev—look, never mind that! You're not going to gammon me, Longe," the baronet said heatedly. "I tell you that you ain't good enough for my niece."

He rounded on Patricia. "Oh, I know what you're

197

going to say. Hey? Charteris is the one who caused the massacre of the Nineteenth. He took me in completely," he added gloomily. "I thought he was a right one and had the Viscount Wellington's ear. Damned scoundrel. Don't know what Delphie saw in him to start with."

"But since you now agree that the colonel is altogether abominable," Patricia began, "surely you see—"

"I don't see nothing that *you* want me to see, and that's a fact," Lord Burgess retorted. "What I feel about the colonel is neither here nor there. Hey? Longe here ordered a retreat. In a word, he ran for it. You can't wrap plain facts in clean linen, my girl. If the colonel's a drunken sot and a liar, Longe is a coward, and I don't know which is worse."

Patricia broke away from Lord Longe and ran across the room to confront her uncle. "Do not be so sheep-brained, I beg! Captain Oranger will tell you that Lord Longe is no coward."

Lord Burgess snorted. "How could Oranger tell me anything? He was lying flat on his back riddled with Frenchy bullets."

Captain Oranger nodded regretfully. "That's the truth, ma'am. I'm sorry to say that I was *non compos mentis* at the time."

"See that? I'm not about," Lord Burgess went on wrathfully, "to give my consent to your marrying this fellow."

"I do not need your consent," Patricia shot back. "You are not the head of my family."

"She has you there, Burgess." Lord Longe grinned.

After glaring at the duke's son, Lord Burgess rounded on his niece once more. "If you think that

Jack's going to consent to having you walk into parson's mousetrap with a ramshackle fellow like this, you've queer in your upper works, my girl. Stop talking slum and have some sense."

The reality of what her uncle was saying hit Patricia almost viscerally. Up until this moment she had never taken into account what Jack might say. But after only a moment's hesitation she rallied. "You do not know that. You are most certainly no judge of character, Uncle Hector. Consider how you allowed yourself to be turned up sweet by the colonel."

Lord Burgess began to swell with indignation, and Lord Longe interposed that he would gladly let Jack Surrey decide the matter. He smiled at Patricia, who took several steps back toward him.

Lord Burgess hastened to wedge his pudgy self between the lovers.

"Don't you come near him, Patricia. He ain't welcome at Burgess Hall, not after all the trouble he's caused me." The baronet pushed his plump face a few inches closer to Lord Longe's adding, "I tell you plain to your head—as long as Jack's not in England, I'm the one to decide who's to pay his addresses to m'niece. And you ain't him."

Lord Longe shrugged. "Then I'll wait for Surrey to return."

Patricia felt another qualm. Jonathan had warned her that there were many who would continue to believe the colonel's lies. Her uncle obviously did so. What would Jack believe?

Jack had been at Talavera. He had been in Lord Longe's regiment. He must have heard the rumors about Lord Longshanks. If he believed them—

"But the rumors are not true," she exclaimed.

"Gammon," her uncle replied glumly. "Where there's smoke there's fire, miss. Things don't happen because you want them to."

He was thinking of his unpaid gaming debts, debts that he had meant Charteris to settle. Of course, he was not so lost to all proper feelings as to wish such a husband on Delphie, but at the same time he was in a devilish coil. He would need to find some way of settling with the vultures, and Maria was bound to kick up dust if he sold the plate or jewels.

And he had Lord Longe to blame for it. If Longe hadn't produced this Oranger fellow from God knows where, all would have been well. Lord Burgess glowered at the duke's son, but Lord Longe did not see that glare. He was aware only of the shadows that were filling Patricia's expressive eyes. She was having doubts again. Perhaps she even believed what her uncle was saying.

Quietly he said, "You must be sure, Patricia. You must believe in me—and in yourself."

"Don't let him gammon you," Lord Burgess warned. "Hey? Have some sense, girl, and—now what's to do?"

A loud clatter was heard in the courtyard followed by a chorus of male voices. "Hillo, hillo, hillo," a cheery voice yodeled. "I say, where are the dashed grooms?"

Lord Burgess started like a hound on the scent. "My son!" he shouted.

As he rushed out of the morning room, Patricia was suddenly filled with a new fear. "It is my cousin Lionel," she cried. "Why has he come back to England so soon? Perhaps something has happened to my brother."

She, too, raced out of the room and flew down the stairs. As she reached the ground floor, footmen swung the front door open allowing two young men to enter the house. One was short, portly, and had a ruddy, merry face, while the other was tall, hazel-eyed, and slender.

"Jack!" Patricia screamed.

Strong arms enfolded her in a warm hug. Patricia leaned into the embrace for a moment then stepped away to look anxiously up at her brother's face. Eyes the mirror image of her own smiled back. There was color in Jack's cheeks, and when Patricia patted his arms, she felt that they were strong and muscular again.

"You have not come back because you are ill?" she inquired anxiously.

Before he could answer, a jovial voice replied, "Rain, Coz."

Lionel sauntered up to Patricia and dropped a kiss on her cheek. "It rained every dashed day we were on the Continent," he said. "Rained in Rome, rained in Florence, rained in dashed Pisa. Frightful place, Pisa. Only thing to look at is a dashed tower, which tilts to one side and makes you dizzy if you look at it long enough. Rum go, if you ask me. Architect must have been disguised. Finally Jack and me had enough and decided to come back to England."

Lionel was interrupted by a shriek from his mother, who came hurrying down the stairs to clasp her firstborn to her bosom. "My dear boy," Lady Burgess declaimed feelingly, "how like you to appear like this and frighten us to death."

"Now don't start on me, Mater." Good-naturedly, Lionel Harmon saluted his mother's cheek. "I've been dashed well rained on for a month, and that's more than the outside of enough. Of course," he added fair mindedly, "it's dashed well raining tonight, too, but it's *English* rain. Makes a difference somehow, though I'm dashed if I know why."

Lionel paused to draw breath and greet Freddy. As he did so, Patricia grasped her brother's arm. "Jack," she whispered, "I must speak with you."

He looked surprised at the urgency in his voice. "Is something the matter?"

She glanced up at the second floor landing, but Lord Longe was not there. Grateful that he had the sense to keep out of sight until she'd had a chance to explain matters to her brother, Patricia hedged, "That depends."

"You're being mysterious, Patty." The use of her nursery name boded well, but much to Patricia's chagrin, there was no chance to be alone with Jack. Lord Burgess's guests were coming down to greet the travelers and demanding that they tell the story of their adventures on the Continent.

Patricia and Jack followed the others back into the great hall. The orchestra hushed, the returning travelers were settled in front of the fire, and servants brought out a large bowl of rumfustian, which had been hastily assembled by the cook. Lionel smacked his lips over this concoction of twelve eggs, sherry, nutmeg, sugar, and lemon rind.

"Nothing like it," he said with deep satisfaction. "I was getting tired of the dashed swill those foreigners drink. No dashed bottom to it, none at all. Give me England any day." He swallowed deeply then added, "But, hillo, hillo, here's something odd. Where's m'sister?"

Freddy promptly volunteered to go and find Delphie. "P-probably admiring herself in the mirror," he added, with a grin. "C-can't be mourning over Charteris's disgrace."

Suddenly conscious of his father's baleful eye, he hurriedly took himself off, and Lionel wondered, "Who's this Charteris and why is he in dashed disgrace?"

Lady Burgess sighed. "Oh, that we ever nourished that viper in our bosom."

Lionel looked bewildered and confessed that he could not make heads or tails out of what his mother was saying. "Are you talking about a dashed snake or a man?" he asked.

While several voices spoke at once explaining the colonel's infamy, Patricia whispered, "Jack, there is something I have to tell you before Uncle Hector speaks of it. It concerns the vile rumors that Colonel Charteris has repeated about—"

A splintering crash outside interrupted her. This was immediately followed by a string of male curses and female shrieks.

Lady Burgess went pale. "We are being invaded!" she gasped. "The French have landed! Hector—do something at once."

"Don't be a fool, Maria. Hey? Of course it ain't the frogs."

At this moment, Miss Wigge's muffled voice could be heard lamenting. " 'Ruin upon ruin, rout upon rout, confusion worse confounded!' He has fallen on 'the thorns of life.' He bleeds!"

"What's the matter with Wiggy?" Lionel wanted to know. "What's all this about rout and ruin and dashed confusion?"

Freddy now reentered the room at a run. "Captain F-Farell's f-f-f—"

Lord Burgess scowled. "Farell! What the devil's he been up to, hey? Spit it out, damn it."

Becoming very red in the face, Freddy produced one word: "Balcony."

"Balcony!" Lionel's round eyes became even rounder. "What's this Farell chap doing on a balcony in the rain and in the middle of the night? Must be a curst rum touch."

Lord Burgess grasped his younger son's shoulders and shook him. "Out with it," he roared.

Freddy made a superhuman effort to be coherent.

"Farell was t-t-trying to lope across the b-border with D-Delphie, but when he tried c-climbing up the l-ladder, it b-broke and down he tumbled. Landed in the r-rosebushes. Pretty thorny place to land, I'll b-be bound."

Chapter Twelve

"**M**y child!" Lady Burgess wailed. "Captain Farell is abducting my child!"

Lord Burgess trundled purposefully for the door. "Call the watch, Charms," he ordered the scandalized butler. "I'll have Farell clapped into Newgate before the night's out."

Lady Burgess seemed inclined at first to faint, but when she saw how her guests followed their host en masse, she reconsidered. With a despairing cry of, "My child!" she also exited.

Lionel sat down and stretched his short, booted legs to the fire. He took another glass of rumfustian and invited the astounded Jack to do the same.

"It's another of Delphie's dashed starts," he explained cheerfully. "Won't come to anything. Warms my heart to see that nothing's changed here at home, Jack, give you my word."

Unable to share this optimistic view, Patricia caught up her skirts and hurried up the stairs to

Delphie's chamber where she found Miss Wigge wringing her hands.

"Oh, Miss Surrey, we are undone," she moaned. "All is lost. 'Oh, that this too, too solid flesh should melt, thaw, and resolve itself into a dew.' "

With some effort Patricia restrained herself from shaking the woman. "Where is my cousin?"

Miss Wigge pointed to the balcony. "He was to ascend like Romeo. Alas, it would have been so exquisitely romantic."

Patricia hurried through the French windows that led to the balcony. Here, unconscious of the fine rain that was falling, Delphie was leaning over the stone wall. She was still dressed in her ball gown, but she had added a French hood that had been fashionable in the sixteenth century and carried a long-stemmed rose in one hand.

When she saw Patricia, she cried tragically, "Oh, Patricia, my life is ruined."

Patricia glanced over the balcony wall. A broken ladder lay along the ruined rose hedge, and Lord Longe was assisting the black-cloaked Captain Farell to his feet. When he looked up, Patricia motioned wildly that he was to keep out of Jack's sight, but his lordship only sent her an airy wave and a smile.

"Oh, heavens, there is Papa," Delphie exclaimed.

Lord Burgess had erupted out of doors. He apparently had seized his riding crop from the hall and was twitching it threateningly against his thigh.

"Just wait till I get my hands on you," he snarled.

He advanced on Captain Farell, who silently continued to pick thorns out of himself.

Delphie leaned over the balcony and shrieked, "You leave him alone, Papa. He has done nothing."

Patricia put a hand on her cousin's arm. "Perhaps you had better tell me the whole, Delphie."

With tears in her eyes Delphie pleaded, "Do not eat me, Patricia. That day in the rose garden I convinced Arthur that I could not *possibly* marry the horrible colonel. Arthur did not want to elope with me, but he realized that I would die of a broken heart if I could not be with him. Finally he agreed to fly with me to Gretna Green."

And Miss Wigge had doubtless helped them plan the details of this idiotish elopement. Patricia noted that under his riding cloak, Captain Farell was wearing trunk hose and a doublet with a lace ruff at the neck.

"Was he really going to travel dressed in that silly costume?" she wondered.

Delphie bridled. "Arthur looks so *well* in doublet and hose. He would have changed later, of course. Oh, it would have been perfect if only the horrid ladder had not broken."

An ominous rumble rose from the ground below. "Well, sir, what have you to say for yourself before I take my whip to you, hey?"

Patricia could not make out the captain's reply, for Delphie screamed and, dodging past her cousin, raced out of her room. Patricia followed, with the ashen-faced Miss Wigge tottering at her heels.

Circumventing the crush of guests by using the side door, Patricia emerged into the courtyard. Rain was still falling, and it puddled about the portly figure of Lord Burgess and the defiant one of the captain. Apparently the latter had just finished speaking, for Lord Burgess was beginning to sputter.

"You're a—a damned nail, sir," he was snarling.

"Accepting the hospitality of my house and plotting to ruin my daughter—"

The captain started as though stung. "No such thing," he protested. "Honorable intentions. Assure you, devote my life to making Miss Harmon happy—would be cut to pieces before hurting her—better marriage to me than bondage to Charteris. Shouldn't speak ill of a brother officer, but—drunken sot. Word of a gentleman—"

"Word of a nincompoop!" Raising his crop, Lord Burgess advanced on the captain, who drew himself up to his full height. But before he could deliver a blow, the baronet found his arm seized.

"You are creating a scandal," Lord Longe informed him. "Haven't you and your precious colonel done enough for one evening?"

"Unhand me, Longe!" the baronet ejaculated. "What d'you mean, interfering with—"

"Think of your daughter's reputation," his lordship interrupted. "Can't you see that your guests are watching you make a fool of yourself?"

Lord Burgess rolled his bloodshot eyes toward the front steps and saw that his guests had gathered there and were watching his antics with lively interest. Some distance away, the grooms, undergrooms, coachmen, and assorted servants were craning their necks to see what was afoot.

Thanks to the efficient Charms, there was light enough for everyone to see by. Footmen held lanterns that shed light on the rainy darkness. This light caught on Delphie's golden hair as she burst out of the house.

She would have run to the captain's side had not Freddy caught her by the waist and hauled her back. "Don't be s-sheep-brained," he admonished. "You'll make a bad thing worse."

Delphie kicked backward and caught her brother on the shin. He howled and let her go, whereupon she ran to her lover's side. "Arthur, has my father hurt you?"

She would have cast herself into his arms, but the captain held her off. "This isn't the time or the place. Best go to your mother, Miss Harmon."

"Good advice," Jonathan said. He struggled between impatience and laughter as he added, "Let be, Burgess. This matter can be talked over quietly."

"Not before I horsewhip this blackguard. As for you, miss, I'll deal with you later."

With her eyes narrowed into obstinate slits, Delphie faced her father. "Papa, if you touch one hair of Arthur's head, I shall enter a nunnery." Lord Longe choked. "Rather than live a life without my love, I will do something dreadful," Delphie insisted.

Everyone began to speak at once. Captain Farell protested his honorable intentions while Delphie repeated that she would forswear the world and enter a convent. Lord Burgess, still restrained by Lord Longe, shouted, "Hey? Hey?" at the top of his lungs. Lady Burgess railed against her ungrateful daughter. Miss Wigge quoted anguished poetry. Lady Were, looking delighted at the thought of the mountains of scandal she had gleaned in one night, wagged her head so hard that she unsettled her purple turban. The ladies exclaimed against the morals of the younger generation, the young ladies giggled over the captain's attire, and the young

209

blades made bets on who would end up horsewhipping whom.

Patricia realized that this was the perfect opportunity to speak to her brother. She saw Jack standing with the others on the porch and had turned to go to him when a young voice exclaimed, "None of you have any s-sense."

Lord Burgess regarded his younger son with loathing. "Did I hear you speak?" he demanded.

That tone of voice usually reduced Freddy to incoherence, but tonight he stood his ground. "I m-mean it, sir," he said. "All this argle-bargle in front of the s-servants and your guests—it's the outside of enough. There's only one person with any s-sense, and it's Lord Longe. You sh-should listen to him."

Lord Burgess was dumbfounded. Not so his wife, who called, "Freddy, you have become feverish while standing in this rain. Mimsby! Go and bring your master back at once."

The valet started forward threateningly, but Freddy rounded on him and shouted, "Go away, Mimsby."

The bully stopped, astonished. "If you come within an inch of m-me," Freddy continued wrathfully, "I'll draw your cork, Mimsby. I've had as much as I'm going to take from you. You're s-sacked."

A cheer rose from the assembled grooms and servants, and Seamus's broad Irish brogue invoked the saints to witness Mr. Harmon had entered into his manhood. Mimsby looked astounded and Lady Burgess mourned, "Now, I know my son has gone mad!"

Ignoring his mother, Freddy faced up to Lord Burgess again. "People have long m-memories, Pater. They'll remember you was friends with Charteris. And after this s-scene tonight, who'll want to offer for a gudgeon like Delphie?"

"Hold your tongue, boy," Lord Burgess exploded.

Freddy blanched and glanced hastily at Lord Longe. Whatever he saw in those gray eyes must have restored his confidence, for he retorted, "No, I ain't going to."

Patricia clasped her hands together and cried, "*Good*, Freddy!"

"Your fault from first to last, Pater," Freddy continued. "Incurring debts and then trying to shackle Delphie to Charteris so you could get out of them. P-people have long memories, and that'll hurt Delphie's chances."

"Not if I can help it," expostulated the captain. "My sword's at her feet. I will never—"

"Best, perhaps, to listen to Farell's suit," Freddy interrupted. "He was born with rats in the upper works, b-but he's a gentleman. Has a decent living from his m-mother and a career in the military. And Lord knows why, but he loves Delphie."

Before Lord Burgess could reply, a cheerful voice issued from the top of the stairs.

"Sounds like dashed good advice to me, Pater. Flighty female, Delphie. Fond of her, mind—my dashed sister, after all—but no peace with all her starts. Last time, it was the dashed dancing master and then the curate and God knows who else. Marriage'll settle her."

Heartened by Lionel's support, Freddy was about to cast himself once more into the breach when a cry from Jack stopped him. "Hell and the devil," he exclaimed.

He was staring fixedly at Lord Longe. Patricia

felt as though she had sustained a blow to her heart. "Lord Longe!" Jack expostulated.

Letting go of the baronet, Lord Longe stepped forward into the light. "Captain Surrey, I think?"

"As if you don't know," Jack shouted. He came down the steps at a run, but found Patricia blocking his way.

"Jack, I must speak with you," she cried.

"Get out of my way, Patricia," Jack gritted. "It's Lord Longshanks."

Despair filled Patricia's soul. In her brother's voice and words she heard her lover's fate. And as though this were not enough, her uncle began to excuse himself.

"Not my fault, Jack, give you my word. Fellow insinuated himself into our company. Hey? We don't receive him here. As to his offering for Patricia—"

"Lord Longshanks wants to marry my sister?"

Jack's voice cracked on a high note of astonishment. It seemed to seal her doom. Heedless of anything and anyone, Patricia clutched at her brother's solid shoulders and attempted to shake him.

"Will you listen to me?" she cried. "I love Lord Longe. I do not care what he is supposed to have done. I love him. And if you forbid me to marry him, I shall do so anyway."

She broke off as strong hands caught her by the shoulders. For a moment she looked up into smiling gray eyes. "A moment, my love," Lord Longe said. "I must have a word with your brother first."

Gently but firmly he set her aside, and he and Jack Surrey faced each other. Then, Patricia's brother gave an exultant shout.

"Lord Longe," he cried. "At last I can thank you properly."

He threw his arms about the duke's son and embraced him. Dizzied with astonishment, Patricia clutched hold of Freddy's arm for support.

"*Thank* him?" Lord Burgess sputtered. "What for?"

Jack stopped embracing Lord Longe and turned a sunshine-bright face to his sister. "Patricia, this is the man who saved my life at Talavera."

She could not speak. She could not think. She could only stare at Lord Longe, who said, "Jack exaggerates. I merely—"

"Exaggerate? But that is like you." Once again, Jack addressed his sister. "Lord Longe is too modest for his own good. He asked all of us in the Nineteenth Foot Guard not to speak of his heroism, and because he'd just saved our lives, we could not refuse him. But now that you're to marry him, I have a right to break my silence."

Lord Burgess looked to be on the point of expiring. "But—but he retreated in the face of fire."

"He got us out of hell," Jack corrected. "Cannon was tearing us apart, and the cuirassiers were thundering down on us. So he called a retreat that saved our lives."

Halfway to the rear Jack had been shot down. "I was in a bad way, but Lord Longe carried me to safety on his back. Then he ordered what was left of the Nineteenth to regroup and face the cuirassiers again. *And* we held them."

As if in a dream, Patricia listened to her brother describing Lord Longe's bold strategy. Far from being the coward of Talavera, he was a man loved and honored by his officers and men.

"Deservedly so," Jack added. "He's the bravest man I know."

"Enough," Lord Longe interrupted. Then, as Jack seemed ready to argue, he added severely, "You've only recently recovered from your wounds. Why are you standing out here in the rain?"

His words recalled everyone to the dismal weather. Lionel promptly retreated into the house for some more rumfustian and was followed by his subdued sister and Captain Farell, by Freddy, who was categorically refusing to give the tearful Mimsby a character, by Miss Wigge, Lord Burgess, his shaken lady, and by all their guests.

Mr. Yancey, however, paused a moment. " 'So faithful in love and so dauntless in war,' eh?" he quoted. "Bedad, I wish you happy, Miss Surrey, though I doubt if Jonathan deserves you. M'homage, ma'am."

He strolled off after the others, but Jack stayed back to ask Patricia, "What did you mean when you said I would refuse to consent to your marrying Lord Longe, Patty? It's the happiest day of my—"

Lord Longe caught the young man by the arm and nodded meaningfully toward the house. Suddenly enlightened, Jack nodded, winked at his sister and strode off toward the house singing the familiar tune with somewhat different words:

> They shout it high,
> They shout it low,
> They shout it far and near-oh.
> Lord Longshanks saved us, every one,
> That day at Talaver-o.

When Jack was out of earshot, Patricia exploded. "*Why?*"

"Why what, my love?"

"Why did you not tell me everything? And pray do not call me 'my love.' I am exceedingly annoyed with you."

He put his arms around her and, in spite of her efforts to free herself, clasped her firmly around the waist. "But I explained all that. Besides, there was my pride. You were so eager to believe Charteris, dear one."

She winced at the truth of this, and he continued, "I was hurt that you could condemn me without hearing my side of the story. I own that I was out of charity with you for an hour or two, Patricia."

The rain had devolved into a soft mist. It obscured Burgess Hall and the rest of the world and gave the illusion that only the two of them existed in the world.

"And after that?" Patricia murmured.

"When I regained my senses, I could understand why you felt as you did. I knew then that I must win your love in spite of Charteris's lies."

He bent to kiss her, but Patricia was not yet ready to be kissed.

"But you could have told me *something* of the truth," she charged. "You could have said that you had saved Jack's life, Jonathan. It would have made all the difference."

He looked suddenly grave. "Yes, I know. Jack told me a great deal about you, you see. If we hadn't met on the downs, I would have come to pay my respects to you. But when I saw you, everything changed. Do you remember how we met?"

She recalled that overcast February day when Argos had tossed her into the mud.

"When I first saw you," Lord Longe went on, "I knew you to be the loveliest woman I'd ever seen and the dearest. I fell in love with you then, completely and irrevocably. I even loved the mud on your cheek."

Gently he touched her cheek with his fingers. "I knew how much Jack meant to you, and I didn't want you to love me out of gratitude. I wanted you to love me unconditionally. As I did you."

Lord Longe wished he could see her face more clearly. He wasn't sure what her silence meant. When that silence stretched on and on, he said, "When you told me the other night that you loved me, I was overjoyed. In spite of yourself, you'd fallen in love with the 'coward of Talavera.' And when you said that you would become Lady Longe—"

She interrupted him at this point. "You are taking a great deal for granted, sir. What you have just told me has changed everything. I believe that I do not *want* to become Lady Longe after all."

He started as though stung. "What's that you say? Patricia, don't trifle with me. What do you mean?"

Even though she was tempted to repay him in his own coin, she could not bear his dismay. Smiling, Patricia reached up and, clasping her arms around his neck, drew his dark head down to hers.

"I mean," she said softly, "that I would much rather be Lady Longshanks."

Regency presents the popular and prolific . . .
JOAN SMITH